FOREVER IN LOVE

THE CITY LOVE TRILOGY

CITY LOVE
LOST IN LOVE
FOREVER IN LOVE

FOREVER IN LOVE

A **CITY LOVE** NOVEL

SUSANE COLASANTI

 KATHERINE TEGEN BOOKS
An Imprint of HarperCollins Publishers

ISBN 978-0-06-230776-7

Typography by Erin Fitzsimmons
17 18 19 20 21   PC/LSCH   10 9 8 7 6 5 4 3 2 1
❖
First Edition

To Katherine Tegen
for all of the possibilities
you bring to life

CHAPTER 1
SADIE

I NEVER KNEW SILENCE COULD be so loud.

This is the loudest silence of all. Buzzing with things left unspoken. Humming with the discomfort of a forced reunion. But here we are. My parents; my brother, Marnix; and me. Having dinner at our small dining room table like we are any other average family. Kind of how we pretended it was before Marnix and I left for college. The throwback tableau appears perfect as long as you don't squint at it too hard.

I can't believe I'm back here in the West Village apartment I grew up in. The one I fled right after I graduated from high school. Even though I moved to another apartment in the same neighborhood, it still counted as a victorious escape. Living with Darcy and Rosanna this summer in our University of New York student housing apartment has been a sweet taste of freedom. Visiting my parents for a few minutes here and there is one thing. But sitting here with them and Marnix at Sunday dinner like the good little family we never were is a joke.

"Can you pass the corn?" Marnix asks Mom.

Mom scrambles to slam down her glass, swallow the water in her mouth without choking, and grab the platter of roasted corn on the cob. Her bustling to give Marnix exactly what he wants, exactly when he wants it, would lead one to suspect that the corn's true identity is a nuclear bomb. If Marnix can't defuse the ticking corn within the next thirty seconds, the entire population of New York City could die.

"This corn is delicious!" Mom gushes. "Best corn of the summer. Nothing beats that farm stand in New Jersey for freshness. Isn't that right, Ron?"

"Best farm stand in Jersey," Dad confirms.

"And the tomatoes! Oh my gosh, Marnix, you should have been here in July. The Jersey tomatoes were bursting with flavor. You could eat them with nothing on them at all. One night we had tomato salads for dinner—just chopped tomatoes, cucumbers, croutons, salt, pepper, and olive oil—and it was unbelievable. The produce has been excellent this summer. Something about the amount of rain we got . . ."

Mom's manic bubble pops when she looks at Marnix and actually sees him. Slumped down in his chair. Clearly wishing he were anywhere but here. There was no way Marnix could have been home in July. He shouldn't even be in New York right now. He should be in Tucson, Arizona, where he goes to college. The next time we should be seeing him is Christmas.

But here he is. Back at the table that's been a part of this apartment since before we existed. Eating Jersey-fresh corn on the cob while Mom's forced conversation glosses over everything that is wrong with this picture. Tonight is Marnix's first night back home. Mom has been acting weird since he got here. She's always been a cheerful person, but anyone could see how fake she's being tonight. She has only touched on upbeat, peppy topics instead of drifting into her usual passionate discussions with my dad about everything from endangered species and the overall destruction of our planet to the increasing prices of health insurance and college tuition. Like she thinks being herself around her own son would send him over the edge. Is she going to walk on eggshells around Marnix until he goes back to Arizona?

"We should do this every Sunday night," Mom says. "Sunday family dinner! Wouldn't that be fun?" She beams at me expectantly. "That way we would be able to see you more when school starts."

"Sunday family dinner." I try to match her enthusiasm. "That would be awesome." There is no way I am playing this twisted game every single week. Marnix won't go for it, either.

"Marnix, what do you think?" Mom asks.

"Might as well." He butters the other half of his corn. Marnix has always eaten corn on the cob this way. He likes to butter one half and eat it before he tackles the other half. "Since this is where I live. Again."

Mom beams some more. "It's only temporary. Just until you get your feet on the ground."

Marnix puts down his butter knife, carefully balancing the blade on his plate with the sharp edge facing away. He looks at Mom.

"Is that what you're calling it?" he says. "Getting my feet on the ground? What does that even mean?"

Mom is startled. "I wasn't . . . I didn't mean anything by it. You can stay here as long as you'd like."

"Okay then," he fires back. "How about not at all?"

"Watch your tone," Dad says. "Your mother is only trying to help you. You should be grateful."

"Grateful?" Marnix snorts. "Helping? How is she helping? By having me committed to a rehab facility? By keeping me prisoner in this apartment for the rest of the summer? By threatening that I might miss next semester if I don't snap out of it? If she wanted to help me, she would leave me alone!"

"That's enough!" Dad yells.

I can hear my heart pounding in my ears. Dad never yells. Except for those scary fights he used to have with Marnix.

"What?" Marnix taunts. "You're going to send me to my room? Don't bother." He pushes his chair away from the table, dropping a summery orange linen napkin from his lap onto the table. "I'm one step ahead of you." Marnix pounds down the hall to his room so heavily that my chair trembles with the vibrating hardwood floors. Then he slams his door.

This whole scene takes me right back to high school. Marnix was always slamming his door back then. It terrified me every time.

When I was a freshman and Marnix was a junior, he started having these enraged fits. One day he was the same quiet boy I'd always known, locking himself away in his room for hours and not speaking to any of us at dinner. Then he changed into a boy who would snap over the most minor thing. He had loud fights with our parents that were so awful I hid in my room. One time I even blockaded my door. Mom said it was hormones. Dad said he'd grow out of it. He never did. His door slamming was usually the beginning of one of his fits. By the time he left for college, I was still scared every time I heard it.

I don't know if he's been different at college. Maybe living away from us in the dorms has mellowed him out. I know I'm a lot more aware of my behavior now that I have two roommates. The last thing I want to do is irritate them in any way. So it's possible Marnix could have calmed down in a new environment with new people.

But even if he did, there was obviously still something wrong.

Marnix tried to kill himself. That's why he was in rehab. That's why he came home.

All I know is that it happened in April near the end of last semester. Mom says she doesn't know why he did it. Apparently Marnix wasn't ready to talk about it during the weekly visits my parents made to his rehab facility upstate, and Marnix's psychiatrist told our parents they shouldn't push him. He said that when Marnix is ready to talk about it, he will come to them.

So this is the first time I've seen Marnix since last Christmas. A sister seeing her brother should be a normal thing. But with us, nothing has ever been normal.

I was so nervous walking over here. I built up an arsenal of things to say, conversation starters to use in case we got lost in awkward silence. We never really talked much before, and we definitely weren't affectionate. But when I put my key in the door and came into the living room tonight, Marnix looked relieved to see me. He jumped off the couch and gave me a big hug.

"Hey, you," he said. "I'm psyched you're here. Mom's acting crazy."

"What else is new?" A smile broke out on my face. I couldn't remember Marnix ever hugging me before. I thought that maybe things would be different now.

But then the fight happened at dinner. And Marnix

stomped away to his room, slamming his door. Same old story.

Marnix's abandoned place at the table is sad. A corner of his napkin fell across the buttered half of his corn when he dropped it. The butter has seeped through his napkin, a dark spot oozing over the bright backdrop.

The dark spot kind of reminds me of my life right now. This summer was supposed to be bright and cheerful. But it is not turning out the way I was expecting. Not at all.

CHAPTER 2
DARCY

THE GUY WHO WAS ALL bossy about ordering his drink gets up in my face.

"This isn't two percent," he accuses.

"Um, excuse me." The lady next in line pierces Bossy Guy with a withering glare far surpassing the intensity of his. He was totally asking for it. When I gave him his drink, he scurried off to his table like a good little customer. But then he hustled back up to the counter like we weren't about to set the world record for Longest Line Ever. The withering glarer was in the middle of ordering when he interrupted her.

"I was here," Bossy Guy tells her. "They messed up my drink." He slams his cup down on the counter. Apparently my identity has been reduced to They, regardless of the name tag on my black tank top that clearly reads DARCY.

"Your drink was made correctly," I say. "With two-percent milk."

"How do you know?"

"I'm the one who made it."

We stare each other down for a few eons. Bossy Guy, infuriated that his pretentious coffee drink was made so skillfully he couldn't tell two-percent milk from whole. Me, aka They, standing strong behind the barista counter, mentally willing him to take his drink back so I don't have to make another one.

Because I'm a barista now. At my job. Where I work.

"Whatever," he growls, snatching the cup back.

"Sorry about that," I apologize to the lady he interrupted. "What would you like?" Her makeup is flawless and she's overdressed for a Sunday. My guess is she won't be staying. She is one of the many New Yorkers zipping through Java Stop on her way to wherever she's already late to, expecting her drink to be ready way faster than it physically takes to make. I never realized how impatient New Yorkers were about their coffee before. And of course I never knew how long it took to make any of these drinks. I've always been on the other side of the counter, ordering my double espresso without thinking about the logistics of not only making it, but making it well.

Until now.

Turns out that when Darcy Stewart is facing a life-or-death situation, she can actually learn how to make something without burning the place down. I was the girl who scorched eggs. I was the girl who set off the smoke detector that one time I was trying to cook dinner. Never in my wildest dreams did I think I would become the girl behind the counter at Java Stop.

And not just any Java Stop. The same Java Stop on Bleecker Street that Sadie protested in front of.

Sadie was devastated when I told her.

"How can you work there?" she wailed. We were having movie night with Rosanna at our place the night I got the job. I was on the couch, Sadie took the puffy armchair, and Rosanna had the violet pouf. "Java Stop is evil. Do you not remember our cardboard sign? Save the West Village?!"

"I didn't have a choice," I apologized. "Trust me, I don't want to be working there any more than you want me to. But they were the only ones who would hire me without previous job experience."

"So . . . are you a cashier, or . . . ?"

"Both. Cashier and barista. Whoever takes the order makes the drink."

"But . . ." Rosanna exchanged a look with Sadie. "No offense, but do they know you're not experienced with making drinks and stuff?"

"Yes. They are training me. Don't worry, they're not

letting me make anyone's drink until I know what I'm doing. The machines do most of the work anyway. How hard can it be?"

Hard. Much harder than I expected. Which is what I found out when I was allowed to start making drinks last week. Fretting over the perfect degree of foam density while a long line of impatient New Yorkers agitating for their caffeine fix are waiting behind you brings stress to a whole new level.

"Here you go." I place Overdressed Lady's small-batch, cold-brewed coffee on the counter. She doesn't tip when she pays for it. I knew she wouldn't. I was surprised to discover that people who look like they can't afford to tip are the ones who tip most frequently.

This line is outrageously long. It's been like this on and off all afternoon. Sadie said Manhattan was empty in August. Is every person not at the beach today here? The only thing getting me through this shift is my plan to meet up with Sadie and Rosanna after work. We're going to walk around and see where the night takes us. Out on the streets, I will feel like myself again.

And that's not all. I am going to tell them why I'm really working at Java Stop. Sadie and Rosanna probably didn't buy the story that Daddy insisted I needed some work experience. That was the only excuse I could think of when I told them I got a job. I've tried to tell them the real reason so many times before. But this is it. They have to know. I have to stop being humiliated about something I can't even control.

At the end of my shift, I burst through the Java Stop door like a prisoner breaking out of jail. Except I will be returning behind bars tomorrow for another day of lattes and long lines.

Rosanna and Sadie are waiting for me at the corner of Barrow Street. Sadie gives me a sympathetic smile.

"How was it?" she asks. She knows I hate working there even more than she hates that I work there.

"Exactly how you think, only worse."

"It kills me to say this, but I do enjoy how you smell like freshly roasted coffee beans after work."

"I know, right?" Rosanna sniffs my shoulder.

"Enough about me." I tap Sadie's arm. "How was dinner?"

Sadie starts walking toward Grove Street, Rosanna and I falling into step beside her. "Oh, I'd say it went about as well as your day," she says.

We wait for her to tell us more. She doesn't.

"How was seeing Marnix?" Rosanna tries.

"Can we . . . maybe talk about this later?" Sadie says. "It was just . . . bad."

"Are you okay?"

"Yeah. But I could really use a walk-and-talk right about now."

"That's what we're here for," I say. I love that Sadie

feels the same way I do about our walk-and-talks. There's something about kicking back with my girls that puts me in a kind of sisterhood love bubble. Three days after Rosanna's meltdown when she hurled clothes and we both hurled insults, she apologized to me. I was so happy we were speaking again that I hugged her immediately. We made up after she told me how hard it was for her to move away from home. I wanted to tell her about Daddy, but his betrayal was too raw for me to even acknowledge what was happening.

I know I can trust Sadie and Rosanna with anything. We've revealed the most vulnerable parts of ourselves to each other. Sadie, sacked out on the couch after she found out Austin was married. Rosanna, whipping the clothes I bought her at me.

And now me. Telling them what really happened.

I start talking before I can wimp out again. "Okay, so . . . remember when my credit card got confiscated? And I thought Logan was messing with me?"

"Uck." Rosanna wrinkles her nose. She and Sadie are disgusted by how Logan played me. "Do we have to talk about him?"

"No. But there is something I need to talk about. It has to do with why I'm working at . . ." I throw Sadie a timid look.

"I knew there had to be a good reason," she says.

"Logan didn't have anything to do with my credit card

being declined. I've been . . . cut off. Financially."

Rosanna slings her arm against my chest to stop me from crossing the street. I'm so frazzled that my brain failed to process the cab barreling toward us.

"What do you mean?" Rosanna asks. She's seen me giving my credit card a workout everywhere from upscale boutiques to the hottest clubs and restaurants. Her brain can't process the concept of Daddy no longer paying my bills any more than mine could process that cab.

"My father was found guilty of tax fraud." Hmm. This is the first time I've used the term *my father* to describe Daddy. It just came out that way. "Can you believe he tried to justify his behavior by complaining how the wealthiest Americans have to support people who don't want to work? Like he was forced to commit a crime because he thought he shouldn't have to pay his taxes? He was only in the highest tax bracket because he had more money than he knew what to do with. But no, apparently he needed more, and lying to the IRS seemed like a more attractive option than paying what he was required by law to pay."

I thought telling my girls about all this would be embarrassing. But I'm not embarrassed. I am so furious I'm shaking.

Sadie puts her arm around me in front of a school on Hudson Street, stepping aside to let a couple walking their dog pass us. "Do you want to sit? There are some good brownstone stoops on Tenth Street."

"No, I'm okay. I want to keep walking. Walking helps. Walking and talking with you guys."

We cross Christopher Street in silence. I can see the Hudson River way at the end of the street, the last colors of sunset fading from the sky. I take a few deep breaths, forcing myself to be in the Now, in this moment when I'm revealing my darkest secret to the girls who are becoming my best friends.

"He got smacked down with fines so huge my mom has to leave our house," I continue. "The bank is seizing it. And I thought having a credit card confiscated was the worst."

"So he's . . ." Sadie searches for the right words. "Is he going to jail?"

"No. His slick lawyer has even slicker connections. But he did have to pay a huge chunk of cash, which was basically all the money he had. Which is why there's nothing left to support me now."

No more unlimited credit card. No more ATM card, either. My parents' joint account was closed. My college fund is protected, but my mom can't afford to send me anything extra. I wouldn't want to take money from her, anyway. She has to sell a bunch of stuff, like furniture and jewelry and dresses, things that are killing her to part with. Apparently when you're married, you are legally responsible for the other person's financial indiscretions. It doesn't matter if you didn't know what they were doing behind your back. So my mom is responsible for paying part of the fines for a crime she didn't even know my dad was committing. How stupid is that? And she has to pay with money she earned from her own catering business. She can't even keep the money she saved from her own job.

"That's so sad about your mom," Sadie says. "You said she has to move out . . . so your dad has to move out, too, right?"

"Are you ready for this?" I warn them. "My dad is moving in with another woman. And her kids."

"What?!" Sadie and Rosanna yell.

"Oh yeah. He's starting a shiny new family and discarding me like some old dishrag. He's actually been seeing this woman for years. I'm sure he couldn't wait for an excuse to leave. I hear she scored a sick estate in Beverly Hills with the money she got from her ex-husband. Guess cheating paid off for her. Not so much for my mom."

I had been clamoring for my dad's attention my whole life. Now I understand why he has never really been there for me. His standard solution to whatever Darcy problem emerged was to throw money at it. He believed that if he threw his money hard enough, the problem would go away.

Now he's out of ammunition.

My dad never focused on me or my mom because his attention was someplace else the whole time. We were only his starter family. Mom doesn't think he would have left us for this other woman if he didn't get found out. She thinks that if he were going to leave us by choice, he would have done it years ago. But Mom didn't give him a choice when she found out about the tax fraud and then found out about the other woman. It was like all her worst fears were confirmed at once.

"I had a feeling there was someone else," she confided when we were talking on the phone last week. She called me when I got home from a double shift where I had to close.

"How did you know?" I asked in a whisper. I was in bed on top of the covers, a sweaty mess since we were cutting back on the electricity bill by not running the air conditioner at night. Rosanna was thrilled I'd adopted her sweat-and-save technique. That was before she knew I didn't have much of a choice. The hot breeze blowing through my windows was doing nothing to cool me off.

"I didn't know for sure," Mom said. "I could never find proof that she was out there. It was just a feeling I'd had for a while. Then there it was. The proof I'd been looking for. I was going through our bills after his fraud was exposed, and I found a separate credit card statement I knew nothing about. Apparently that's the card he used when he was . . . with her."

I could not believe what I was hearing. My father was a manwhore. He was charging all this stuff on the low for this other woman—hotels, extravagant dinners, flowers, drinks at hipster bars like he was twenty-five instead of old. It occurred to me that he was having a midlife crisis. Or maybe he had a brain tumor. But no. He was just an asshole.

Mom's voice was trembling. "How dare he have a secret credit card on top of stealing from his own family—stealing *my* money—and tearing us apart? He used to take me out to the places he takes her. He used to buy me flowers. He treated me like the woman he was in love with. But all that stopped a long time ago. Now I know why." She took a sip of something. I pictured a big glass of red wine. My parents had a huge wine collection. No doubt Mom needed a big old drink . . . or ten. She was probably doing her best to drink up their collection before it was confiscated along with everything else. "I shouldn't be telling you all this."

"No, it's okay," I said. "Tell me anything you want."

"I might be a little tipsy."

"Mom. I'm here. I'm listening."

She took another sip. "You know how sometimes you think it's you? At first I thought it was me, that something was wrong with me. Or that this is what happens after a while with marriages. I mean, how long can romance be sustained? It goes out the window pretty quickly. I thought maybe I wasn't trying hard enough to keep him interested."

Um. Maybe she had a point about too much information.

"But it wasn't about me," she continued. "It was all about her. He was exhausted around me from working so hard to keep her happy." Mom made a bitter snorting sound. "Every time I asked him to take me out in the exact ways he was taking her out, he said he was too tired. Or he had to work late. Or that wasn't his scene anymore. So now we're getting divorced, my savings are gone, and you had to get a job. How's that for a twist?"

Mom was right. I never saw any of it coming. Neither of us did.

We walk along a few blocks of West 10th Street. The air is rich with savory cooking smells from Rosemary's. Every table outside is taken. A cute black bulldog is sprawled on the sidewalk next to one of the tables, his leash looped around his owner's chair. He has a doggy dish of water next to him. His tongue flops out as he looks up at us.

"I'm so sorry you're going through all this," Sadie tells me. "Is there anything we can do to help?"

"Thanks, but I'm okay. I just wanted you guys to know what was going on." There's more that I'm still keeping to myself, though. The harsh truth is, I have no idea if I'm going to make enough to support myself this year. We might be keeping our apartment for freshman year, but we won't find out until later this month. I won't be able to stay if I can't afford the rent. Rosanna has financial aid and Sadie's parents help her out, but what do I have? I will have to cut way back on my Java Stop hours when classes start. There is a scary chance I might have to move to like a borough. Which means I really should break out a map and find out what's near lower Manhattan. Or upper Manhattan might work. That night Logan re-created our first three dates and we rode up to Inwood on his motorcycle, I was surprised by how green and spacious that whole area was. Rents are supposed to be way cheaper up there. The farther you move from the Village/Tribeca area or the bottom half of Central Park, the cheaper rents become. But if I can't swing staying in Manhattan, I am not at all looking forward to living past the last stop on the Z train. And what if I need to get new roommates? The thought of leaving Sadie and Rosanna is so sad I can't even.

Up ahead is some venue with crowds standing around a roped-off entrance. I can't tell what this place is. Maybe a hotel? From the limos out front and heavy security, it's obvious they are having an exclusive event with famous types. Guys in black suits with earpieces are everywhere. Just as we're coming up on the entrance, flashes of paparazzi cameras start popping in a frenzy. Some celeb who just got out of a car must be surrounded by handlers. Paps are holding their huge cameras above the crowd, trying for a killer shot. The prey gets ushered inside so swiftly we can't see who it is. Normally I would ask one of the gawkers who that was. But tonight I don't even care. It's amazing how your priorities can change in the blink of an eye.

I remember that fight Rosanna and I had the night she

blew up at me over being a slob. I said the only problems in life are the ones we create. Now I see how stupid I was. My dad having an affair had nothing to do with me. His tax fraud had nothing to do with me. But now I'm the one left to pick up the pieces. I'm the one scrambling to get by. At least summer session ended this week and I can work extra shifts before fall semester starts. My college fund is protected because it's legally in my name, so thankfully my tuition is covered. But I have to find a way to pay for everything else.

Sadie says that every negative situation has a positive side. I guess the positive side of my life being turned upside down is that I'm being forced to figure out how to survive on my own. But refraining from buying cute bags and dresses and shoes has not been an easy adjustment. Same with not being able to treat friends. And I wasn't expecting my first job to be some minimum-wage deal entirely unrelated to my future career. Although I guess handling characters like Bossy Guy and Overdressed Lady is good public relations training . . .

This life thing just got real.

CHAPTER 3
ROSANNA

THE WHOOSH OF AIR AGAINST my face.

Motorboats putting along the river.

Snippets of classical music coming from somewhere on the grass as a woman does Tai Chi.

A single basketball bouncing on the court.

These are the sounds of running along the Hudson River. They have become familiar to me, sounds I rely on as part of my new routine. I love these early morning runs by myself. D was right. This is the best time to run, when the air is fresh and the park is empty.

Running when you are not a natural runner comes with a set of steep challenges. It feels like every part of my body is fighting against gravity. The sharp stitch in my side. How my lungs feel like they are going to explode. Parts of me I didn't even know were jiggly jiggle. Every step is this huge effort to propel my body up and forward. My body prefers to be grounded. But if I want to be a runner, I have to push myself to do better.

Sometimes it feels like I have to work harder than other people. Even to do something simple like running.

The runners I pass every morning have become as familiar as the sounds of Hudson River Park. You have to be serious about fitness if you're dragging your tired butt out of bed this early in the morning. It helps that I'm a morning person. But what forces me out of bed early is my desire to be like the real runners I see out here every morning. First of all, they are in ridiculous shape. You know you're doing something right when other people can see a bunch of your muscles flexing when you run. I don't want to be the tall, gawky girl fighting gravity. I want to be a graceful, buoyant girl gliding along like the pros.

Initially I wanted to get good at running for D. The first time he took me running was really frustrating. I felt like I was going to throw up after like thirty seconds. There was this shade of disappointment over his eyes when I had to stop and he turned to look back at me, checking to see if I was okay. D is so good to me. The least I could do was get good enough at an activity we could do together. At first my goal was to run with him like a normal person. But now running is more about me. I want to be a runner to feel good about myself. And I have gotten better at it. Now I can run one whole mile before I start slowing down. I can feel myself getting stronger, healthier. My body isn't fighting as hard as it used to. I am acclimating, making smoother motions, bouncing up higher against the downward force.

I have also discovered a kind of mental clarity that comes when I start my day by running. Normally I'm a wreck. My mind starts shooting worries into my mental bulletin board with an industrial electric stapler the second I wake up. But running soothes me. It lets me be right where I am, almost as if everything stressing me disappears for half an hour. I can be free when I run. I can be the Shiny New Rosanna I came here to be.

Darcy likes to talk about being in the Now, and maybe this is what she means. Clearing your mind to just be in the moment and appreciate where you are.

I cross the highway and swing down Charles Lane. Before I run home and get ready for camp, I take a minute to look around me. To completely absorb my surroundings. I am here in New York City. That extraordinary reality hits me all over again. After dreaming of living here for so long, sometimes I'm still shocked that any of this is happening. That I am making it happen.

The rush of my shiny new life has me floating on a natural high all day. When D opens his apartment door that night, the rush hits me stronger than ever.

"Hi!" I can tell my smile is radiating. My smiles typically

do not radiate. Incessant worrying tends to limit the radiance of a smile.

"Hi!" D laughs. "You're in a good mood."

"Life is good." I kiss him on my way in, taking off my battered old black flats and putting my bag on a bench near the door.

"Do you want some water?" D asks. He goes behind the long, sleek island of his open kitchen, taking two glasses out of a cabinet.

"With crushed ice, please."

D gives me a look like, *duh*. How lucky is he to have a refrigerator that makes crushed ice? Rich people really do live in a whole other world.

I sit down on a stool at the island. D puts my glass of water with crushed ice in front of me. He adds a wedge of watermelon to the rim of the glass.

"So why is life good today?" D sits at the island across from me with a glass of water that doesn't have watermelon.

"Running makes me happy," I share.

"That's awesome. I was hoping it would, but I wasn't sure you'd ever get into it."

"Oh, it's on. Early morning running is my thing."

"I can't believe you've been cheating on me with running," D teases. We run together some mornings, and some mornings I run alone.

"I can almost run like a normal person now. But it's

more than just the running. It's like . . . everything is falling into place. I was looking around this morning at how sparkly the sunlight was on the river, listening to the birds chirping, and just absorbing everything around me. It was incredible." I sound like Sadie. Maybe her optimism is finally gaining on my cynicism. "Did you ever have one of those days when everything clicks?"

D smiles. "Oh! That reminds me!" He dashes to the back of his apartment. Then he comes right back with his cell phone. He yells, "Surprise!" and hands it to me.

I look at the screen. It's blank. "Did you want to show me something?" I say. "I don't think it's on."

"No, it's for you."

"What is?"

"My phone. I'm giving you my old one. I just got the new version."

Whoa. "I can't take your phone."

"You have to," D insists. "I'm giving it to you."

"But how can I . . ." I almost ask how I can afford it. From what Sadie told me when I asked about her phone, the bills aren't cheap.

"There's this obscure carrier that charges a low monthly rate," D explains so I don't have to ask. "You're good to go on my plan until the end of the month. Then you can transfer to a plan with them. See . . ." He taps the screen a few times until a memo list comes up. "I put their info here for you."

My throat gets tight. D has already been extremely generous in treating me to things I can't afford. Now he's giving me his phone? It's like he's too good to be true.

"This is . . . thank you." I can't even string together a coherent sentence.

"You're okay with having a cell phone, right?"

"Yeah." I put the phone down on the counter and reach up to hug him, pressing my cheek against his chest. "Thank you so much. For everything."

The second I admitted to D why I didn't have a cell phone, I wanted to take it back. I worried that it was too much too soon, especially after telling him I was molested. But he turned out to be cool with my background. He didn't make me feel ashamed of growing up in a family so poor we couldn't afford a lot of things other people considered givens, like smartphones and cable and senior trips. I can't believe I was questioning whether he was the right person for me. He has been so supportive and understanding about everything.

"Here." D picks up the phone and reaches out his hand for mine, leading me over to his couch. If *couch* is the correct term to describe a fifteen-foot sectional sofa. "Let me show you some features." He sits right next to me, pressing his leg against mine. My leg tingles with electric sparks.

On his phone, D switches the music playing on his overhead sound system to the Ethan Cross station. He knows Ethan Cross has been my husband since eighth grade and he's okay with that. I mean, he even supports my fantasy husbands. D shows me how I can track my health stats when I'm running, how to keep track of my expenses in an accounting app I will definitely be using, and how to update my contacts. Although I have mixed feelings about conforming to society in such a predictable way, not having a cell phone was getting harder to manage every day. People do have a point when they ask what I would do if there's an emergency. My answer used to be that I would borrow someone's phone. But as a person who always has a Plan D (as a backup to Plans A, B, and C), I am hyperaware that anything could happen at any time. And not in a good way.

Except for this. Right here. Us. D knows who I used to be. He knows the past version of myself I am beginning to reinvent and he still wants to be with me. I can't remember the last time I was this happy.

"Any other questions?" D asks after he's shown me the essentials.

"Just one." I kiss him. Then I kiss him again.

He grins. "That's not a question."

"Okay, here's a question. Why are you so good to me?"

D slides his fingers through my hair, capturing me in his laser focus. The intensity in his eyes makes my heart race.

Is he finally going to tell me he loves me?

"Because I care about you," he says.

Now D is the one kissing me. Eventually he presses me down on the couch. Gently. Everything gently. He has been extra cautious about taking things slowly since I told him why it's not easy for me to be physical.

D stops kissing me to lock eyes. His laser focus is more intense than ever.

"You're amazing," he whispers.

Here in his arms, in his home, in the city where I belong, I believe him.

CHAPTER 4
SADIE

CHAPTER 7 OF *YOUR DREAM Life* is all about identifying your most important goals, then making a plan to take steps every day toward achieving them. *Your Dream Life* is this self-empowerment book I've been working with for the past two weeks. I can definitely feel the techniques I've learned starting to work. Instead of just projecting an optimistic attitude to the world and hoping that my underlying anger will eventually fade away, I can feel myself becoming the true optimist I want to be.

I reach over to my nightstand for the cold glass of watermelon juice Rosanna poured me. Before she left for Donovan's, she juiced an entire watermelon in the old blender my mom gave us. Rosanna was not kidding when she told me she developed a new addiction to watermelon juice during her South Beach vacay with D. Now she has me hooked, too.

Your Dream Life wants me to write down my top three goals. I tap my red Gelly Roll Stardust pen against the page. This book isn't only perfect for working on short- and long-term goals, it's helping me research my future career. I want to be an urban designer focusing on holistic wellness living. Austin opened me up to that aspect of urban design.

He opened me up to a lot of things. . . .

When Austin brought me to the *LOVE* sculpture and gave me that warm fuzzy he made, I could have forgiven him for everything. There are so many reasons why I love him. One is that he notices the details. Boys aren't usually the best at that, but Austin noticed the tiny *LOVE* sculpture replica I put on my desk at the beginning of the summer when my internship started. He noticed, then he made a grand gesture that swept me away.

I put my book down to check the time. If I don't put my laundry in the dryer right now, someone might dump my wet clothes out so they can use the two washing machines my colors and lights are occupying. That's already happened once this summer and once was more than enough. When the laundry dumper tossed my wet clothes on the folding table, they either didn't notice or didn't care that some of them fell on the floor amid the dust bunnies and grime. I came down to the laundry room only ten minutes after my wash stopped. The punishment did not fit the crime.

Flying down the stairs, I have a feeling I forgot something. My relief at finding my wet clothes still in the washing machines is replaced with annoyance when I remember that my laundry card is twenty-five cents too short to run the dryer. That's what I was supposed to remember. To add more money to my laundry card online. But then I lost myself in my book. I decide to transfer my wet clothes to the dryer while I'm down here so they don't end up on the floor again. I'll come back in a few minutes to get the dryer running.

Back upstairs on my laptop, I go to the laundry service site and sign in. I'm just finishing the card refill when my phone rings. Of course it's Brooke. She likes to call instead of text.

When we hang up half an hour later, I remember my wet clothes sitting in the dryer. I grab my card and race downstairs, feeling like a hypocrite. People who leave their laundry in the machines for hours are just plain rude, and now I'm one of them.

Someone is in the laundry room when I get there. A boy is digging through a towering pile of rumpled clothes and eating Spree. I've seen this boy before. He's the boy my panties went flying at when we were both doing laundry at the same time.

"Hey!" he says.

I try to play it off like he never commented that I had panties like his girlfriend's. Ones with little peace signs. I try not to blush, but when I look at him all I see are flying panties.

"How's it going?" I ask, checking that my wet clothes are still in the dryer.

"Not bad. You?"

"Still wildlife free." When I met this boy in June, he told me that the building used to have an indoor wildlife problem, but it was fumigated last summer. Indoor wildlife does not work for me. As someone who grew up in New York City, maybe I should no longer be scared half to death by a mouse darting across the baseboards or a roach skittering down the wall. But indoor wildlife never gets less terrifying.

"You should be good," he says. "But if you ever have a problem, you know where to find me." He lives below us in 3A.

"We're not too loud, are we? The people above us are like a herd of elephants."

"I never hear you. You're the perfect upstairs neighbors."

"Good." I start the dryer.

"Laundry Procrastinator, right?"

"Sorry?"

"That's how you introduced yourself when we met."

"Oh yeah! And you were Glutton for Punishment!"

"Nice to meet you again. I'm Jesse."

"Sadie."

"Cute name."

I blush a little. Why am I getting a flirty vibe from him? He has a girlfriend. "Okay, well . . . see you around."

"One more thing," Jesse says. "Do you have any single friends who might want to go to this party with me? We're all supposed to bring someone single and then see if we like anyone there. I know it's lame, but my friend is making me go."

"I thought you had a girlfriend."

"Not anymore." Jesse shrugs with a sweet smile. "Her choice, not mine."

"I'm sorry to hear that."

"Don't be. If you're not with someone who loves being with you, what's the point?" Jesse throws some of his clothes into a washing machine. "I want to be with a girl who appreciates my laundry skills. Look, I'm separating the colors and everything." He gives me another sweet smile, adorably proud of his domestic accomplishment.

That's when it hits me. Jesse might be good for Vienna. She and I have been walking together in the annual Remembrance Walk ever since I was thirteen and she was fourteen. Even though we bond like sisters every year, I've never seen Vienna any other time. I'm not really sure why. Maybe because extending our relationship beyond that one day would make what happened to my sister more real? Telling everyone about her is not something I'm ready to do. But there's no reason I couldn't get in touch with Vienna and ask if she wants to go to this party with Jesse. At the walk this year, Vienna told me that she liked a good friend of hers, but she didn't want to tell him how she really felt and risk ruining their friendship. If she didn't tell him or he didn't feel the same way, she might like Jesse. She is adorable and so is he. I don't know; it's like they have the same kind of energy. They remind me of each other in a way I can't explain. Plus they both like Spree, which is an odd candy to have in common. I'm taking the Spree as a sign.

"I think I might have a friend who would go," I say. "Let me find out for you."

"Yes." Jesse pulls his fist down in a *score* gesture. "You rule, Sadie. Thank you."

"No promises or anything. But . . . I think it might work out."

Later when I'm folding my clean clothes on my bed, I think about why I didn't say I'd go to the party with Jesse. He's cute. And funny. And he has the sweetest smile. It's not even about him. It's about keeping an open mind. Who knows who I would meet at that party? Anyone could be there. Anyone could be right around the corner. . . .

But that's my whole problem. I had been looking for a soul mate forever. Then I found Austin. I thought the search was over. Even after everything that happened, I'm wondering if I should keep looking for something I've already found.

One good reason is that Austin is not who I thought he was.

I didn't think I wanted to give Austin another chance. I didn't know if I could trust him again. The day after *LOVE*, I called him and told him I needed some time to think about it. Then I realized something. We had connected so intensely in such a short period of time that what was happening between us was out of his control. Even if he never spoke to me again, our connection would still be real. He would always know that what he had with his wife should have been so much more. That he deserved so much more.

Austin went above and beyond apologizing to me. He felt sick about not telling me he was married. About what he did to her. To us. He moved out, and now he is staying with his friend Trey in Brooklyn. He even filed for divorce.

So I decided to forgive him.

I finish my laundry and go back to my book until I leave to meet up with Austin for dinner. The book is helping me think about my future, but I still don't know if that future will have Austin in it. I'm so lost in thought that I don't even notice a woman is waiting outside my building. She stares at me as the front door swings shut behind me.

I stare back.

"Are you Sadie?" she asks.

I nod. A sinking feeling in my stomach tells me who she is before she does.

"I'm Austin's wife," she says. "I thought we should talk."

CHAPTER 5
DARCY

THINGS LOGAN DOESN'T KNOW I know:

- He came here to scam me out of money to pay off his gambling debt.
- He has been stringing along some beach bimbo this whole time.
- He is going to break up with me as soon as he gets back to California.

I don't think so.

Fool me once, shame on me. Fool me twice, you will reap my wrath.

Logan knew me when I was a wild child in Santa Monica. He was totally down with my self-destructive tendencies. Most weekends we would stay out partying all night. Despite my parents' threats, even a few school nights were casualties. I vaguely remember dragging my sorry ass to class the morning after a particularly rambunctious night, deluding myself that no one could tell I was toasted. Logan excelled at scoring certain alcoholic enhancements and I excelled at sampling them.

Playing with adult beverages was a disaster. I was so wild at one point my parents threatened to send me away to reform school if I didn't shape up. Like I could instantly flip the switch on what was driving me to self-medicate. But their threat of sending me away was enough to get me back on track.

Getting drunk and acting crazy was my way of scoring attention from my dad. It didn't matter that the attention I got was angry, usually involving a lot of yelling on his part. At least he was looking at me. At least my existence was on his radar. One could argue that productive accomplishments would have been a better way to go. But I wasn't aware that I was craving his attention back then. I wasn't thinking rationally. I didn't want to think at all. I just wanted to numb the pain.

Now I want to numb the Daddy pain all over again. And numb the Logan pain while I'm at it.

You could say I've been on a bit of a bender. Okay, fine. A full-on bender of monstrous proportions. Does a bender even count if you're hiding it from your roommates? When I get wasted, I either stay out all night or come home after Sadie and Rosanna are asleep. They assume I'm tired the next day from all the Java Stop/Logan drama.

And no one's complained about me at work, so I guess I'm pulling it off.

Logan hasn't said one word about the wild child's triumphant return. He doesn't love me. If he did, he would be trying to protect me from myself.

Not that I'm even seeing Logan anymore. I've been blowing him off for the past two weeks, ever since I discovered his hideous intentions to manipulate me. He will not be allowed to hustle Darcy Stewart ever again. But I am aware I can't fend him off forever. So far I've been making up excuses to not see him, everything from working double shifts to final exams. But now that summer session is over and he knows where I work, I am going to have to face him.

My initial impulse was to unleash a torrent of revenge so furious that Logan would be scarred for life.

Sadie talked me down from that ledge.

"What do you think that would do for your karma?" Sadie asked from the turquoise beanbag on my floor.

"Muuphhh," I went from under my pillow. Sadie was glued to the couch for days when she found out the truth about Austin. Her anguish must have been contagious. Hiding in bed was my most alluring option after uncovering Logan's dirty secrets.

"Good answer," Sadie said. "But no. Your diabolical plot would destroy your karma. You're better than that. You don't have to stoop to his level. Take the high road.

The best revenge would be to show him you're over him. Like he's so unimportant he doesn't deserve your anger. If you can't be kind to someone who betrayed you, don't interact with him at all." She sounded like one of those self-help books she was always reading.

I slid the pillow off my face. It was getting hard to breathe.

"He's not worth your time or energy. He's just not worth it."

Sadie went on to make a lot more good points. So that's where I am. Avoiding. Numbing. Waiting.

When I moved to New York at the beginning of the summer, this city was a glittery carousel twirling with potential boy adventures. It was a playground that never closed, brimming with endless possibilities for amusement. I want to get back to that fun place. I want to live in that time again. Before Logan came here to supposedly win me back. Before I turned Jude against me.

That is why I'm out tonight. By myself. On the prowl.

Lit Lounge is jumping for a Monday night. Probably because they're having an all-ages event. I've been chilling at the bar, perusing the boys and weighing my options. Three guys have hit on me in the past hour. None of them were my type (i.e. hot, under twenty-five, charming without trying to be). My aversion to cheesy pickup lines didn't exactly motivate them to stick around.

The bartender just sneaked me another strong drink.

Either he wants to hook up with me or he is showing me sympathy for enduring the unwelcome advances of losers. Or both.

"Insomnia!" someone yells at me over the music. He's squeezing his way next to my bar stool, a cute boy who must have just gotten here. Something about him seems familiar. I examine him more closely because I know I would have given him a second glance if I'd seen him before.

"Excuse me?" I yell back, playing along.

"Insomnia Cookies!"

"I love those!"

"I remember!"

That's it. That's where I know him from. Sadie took me to Insomnia Cookies on my birthday. This boy was scrunched up against the tiny counter, wolfing down cookies with another guy. The microscopic store was so crowded that I got shoved into him.

"Hey!" I give him a big hug like we're long-lost friends. I'm not drunk yet. But the drinks from my bartender friend are helping to speed that along.

He laughs, showing his perfect straight white teeth I remember noticing at Insomnia.

"Good to see you!" he yells.

"Totally!"

"Do you come here a lot?"

"First time!"

"Nice! A Lit virgin!"

"What about you?"

"No, I'm not a virgin! I mean to here! But also in life! Am I completely screwing this up?"

He is adorable.

"I come here all the time!" he yells. "I live a few blocks away."

"This place is cool!"

"I know!" He juts his chin at my glass. "You've discovered the secret to all-ages night!"

"What's the secret?"

"You get the hard stuff if you're a pretty girl!"

The stool next to mine frees up when a girl in this season's Manolos leaves. Those shoes were on my want list. I stare at her as she walks away in heels I was meant to wear but can't buy anymore. With every step she takes, my new reality sinks further in. I take a few gulps of my mojito.

Insomnia Boy takes the free stool. He moves it close to mine so we don't have to yell anymore.

"Who are you here with?" I ask.

"My buddies over there." He gestures to the back room. "They won't miss me."

"Who says you'll be gone?"

"Oh snap! So I can't sit with you?"

"Only if you want to."

"I want to."

"Smart choice."

The bartender comes over. Insomnia Boy orders a Coke. I polish off the rest of my mojito. This is my second one and they were both *strong*. Bring on the numb.

"May I buy you another drink?" He flashes that nice smile again.

"If you insist."

The bartender brings Insomnia Boy's Coke. He orders me another of what I was having. Strong mojito number three, coming right up.

"So how was your birthday?" he asks.

"How did you know it was my birthday?"

"Your friend told the cashier. Or did she just say that to get a free cookie?"

"No, it was. It was fun. My friend Sadie took me out."

"For a birthday cookie?"

"I didn't want cake."

"Why not?"

Explaining why I wanted to forget it was my birthday is not part of tonight's festivities. Tonight is all about Summer Fun Darcy getting her latest boy adventure on.

"The cookies were way more appealing," I say. "Did you not smell that place? One sniff gave me a sugar contact high."

The bartender puts my mojito in front of me with a wink. The wink is either cheering me on or competing to stay in the picture. Hard to tell now that I'm buzzed. Everything is blurry around the edges.

"Still," Insomnia Boy says, picking up his glass. "You should let me take you out for cake sometime. No birthday cake on your birthday? That is just wrong."

Another mojito, two Cokes, and one phone number exchange later, we are practically telling each other our life stories. Or maybe it's only me. Through my haze, I'm vaguely aware that I'm doing most of the talking. But I can't tell for sure. The blurry edges are spreading.

"So what if I like to drink?" I hear myself say. "I don't even care anymore. What's the point of playing by the rules if it got me nowhere? What's the point of planning anything? You think things are going one way, and then *blam*!" I attempt to slam my fist into my palm, missing and practically hurling myself off the stool in the process. Insomnia Boy reaches out to steady me.

"You okay?" he asks.

"I'm fabulous. What was I saying?"

"'And then *blam*!'"

"Right. You think things will always be the same, and then your entire life changes overnight. Your dad rips apart your family. The boy you thought wanted you back turns out to be playing you. And the boy you really want never wants to see you again."

Insomnia Boy looks over at the back room where his friends are. The light of recognition in his eyes is long gone. Along with his interest. Even in my tipsy fog, I know he will never call.

But it doesn't matter. Because when my cloudy judgment clears, nothing will be hiding the truth. That there's only one boy I really want. And my chances with him are destroyed.

CHAPTER 6
ROSANNA

"HERE," MOMO SAYS. SHE MADE this jewelry box at the beginning of the summer. Shirley, the arts and crafts director, put some of the boxes on display. Shirley gave back all the projects she put on display now that summer is almost over.

"It's so pretty." I admire Momo's enthusiastic use of pink rhinestones and purple glitter.

"It's for you," Momo says.

"What?"

"Every girl should have a jewelry box. Remember?"

Of course I remember. That's what Momo told me right here on this same bench in the courtyard when she was decorating it. She asked me if I had a jewelry box, and I admitted that I'd never had one. Momo found that to be unacceptable. There is nothing like an eight-year-old to remind you of what your priorities should be.

"I felt bad you didn't have one," Momo says. "So you can have mine."

"But this is your jewelry box. Didn't you say your old one was taken away?"

"Yeah. But I got over it. This one is for you." Momo pulls on the top right side of her T-shirt where a sticker that says GIRL POWER! is proudly displayed. The younger girls had an empowerment workshop this morning. They got cute stickers and notebooks at the end. "You know how we learned about strong girl role models?"

"Yeah?"

"You're mine."

A significant amount of willpower goes into restraining myself from bursting into tears.

Momo puts the jewelry box in front of me on the table. "Don't forget to hide something special in the secret compartment," she instructs. "And you might want to put more glue on this heart rhinestone." She wiggles one of the pink hearts, which is a little loose.

I don't know what to say. "Thank you so much. This is really nice of you."

For a second it occurs to me that she's giving me her jewelry box because she knows I went to her apartment to check up on her. Is this her way of saying thank-you? But I'm not sure if she knows. Momo hasn't said anything about it.

Frank hasn't said anything, either, because he is the lamest camp director of all time. I told him I suspected Momo was being abused, but he didn't do anything. He still hasn't. That's why I decided to take matters into my own hands. Visiting Momo's home was the first step. I don't know what I'm going to do next. But when I have an opportunity to find out what's happening with her, I will jump on it. I would do anything to help her.

Momo goes back to working on her sand bird. Everyone has clear plastic bottles they are filling with colored sand. Shirley showed the kids how to make the colors of sand appear in thin or thick stripes. Then she expertly tilted the funnel in the bottle she was using to make her stripes zigzag. The completed sand birds will have googly eyes, feathers, and a yellow golf tee for a beak. I remember making one of these when I was little, except with a glass bottle.

Jenny uses the last of the pink sand. She's sitting on the other side of Momo. This is how we've been sitting in arts and crafts every day: Jenny, then Momo, then me. The four other girls in my group are on the bench across from us. Momo doesn't even have to ask me for more pink sand. Her love for pink is extreme and unwavering. I ask if anyone needs anything. Then I go up to the hut for more sand.

The service window where Shirley gives us materials is closed, which is weird. Usually Shirley keeps it open all day. Same with the door on the side of the hut, where

Shirley is usually dashing in and out, distributing supplies and complimenting the kids on their projects.

I look around at the tables for Shirley. She's not out here. Should I knock on the window? Instead, I go right to the door.

I knock.

No one answers.

I knock again, louder.

Still nothing.

Shirley was just at the tables a few minutes ago. She was handing out more golf tees. She's got to be around here somewhere.

When I try the doorknob, it turns smoothly. I push the door open and walk in.

At first I don't see her. It's more like I sense someone is in the room. But then I see Shirley in the corner, sitting on the cement floor, wedged between some shelves and the wall.

Crying.

"Are you okay?" I ask, darting over to her. "What happened?"

"I'm okay," Shirley says. She wipes tears from her face in quick strokes, pushing up from the floor. "Sorry about that. Did you need something?"

"What's wrong?"

She jams her lips together, trying not to cry. "Sorry. I just need a minute. I'll be right out."

"You don't have to apologize. I want to help you. What can I do?"

"No one can help me." Shirley presses her fingertips against her eyelids. "No one can fix this. Not even me."

"Did something happen with one of the kids?"

She drops her hands and shakes her head, trying for a smile. It looks as broken as she must feel. "No, this has nothing to do with camp. My husband and I are . . . having problems."

My eyes cut to her wedding ring. Have I ever noticed her ring before? Did I know she was married and somehow forgot? I don't think she ever mentioned her husband.

"I'm sorry to hear that," I say. "Are you sure there isn't anything I can do?"

Shirley gets up and goes over to the service window. She lifts it open. "You can help me bring out more sand. Was there a color you needed?"

As I help Shirley bring out more containers of sand, I can't help but wonder what kind of problems she's having with her husband. Shirley is really young to be married. I know she's twenty-one. She must still be in college, unless she doesn't go to college. Shirley and her husband must have really been in love to get married so young. But maybe their love is changing. Or maybe it's not what they thought it was.

"Here you go." I put a container of pink sand on the table in front of Momo.

She grins at me. "How did you know I wanted more pink sand?"

"Because I know you." I sit down next to her, watching all my girls put the finishing touches on their sand birds. "These are fabulous," I announce. "You girls should start a sand bird business."

"We totally should!" Jenny agrees. She taps the GIRL POWER! sticker on the back of her hand. "If we start planning now, we could throw a fund-raiser when school starts. What should we call our company?"

As the girls brainstorm ideas, the sweet sisterhood moment with Momo giving me her jewelry box and the startling discovery of Shirley crying on the floor collide in an odd mixture of feelings. I am grateful but also upset. It's strange how two feelings so different can inhabit your body at the same time, competing against each other to see who wins. Or maybe it's not a competition at all. Maybe there are times you are meant to feel happy and sad together, even if you don't know why yet.

CHAPTER 7
SADIE

COFFEE SHOP IS USUALLY PACKED all night. Just like it is right now, on a Tuesday night at eleven. A lot of places around here are on the emptier side in August. But Coffee Shop is stuffed with regulars and tourists. We were lucky to snag a window booth.

Rosanna agreed to midnight pancakes as long as we get home before one. She's even having pancakes with us this time instead of her usual two eggs/potatoes/toast dish, which is a few dollars less than pancakes. Rosanna is the most frugal person I know. Darcy could definitely pick up a few tricks from her expert saving skills.

"Something happened last night," I say after the waitress crams our table with plates of fluffy blueberry pancakes, coffees, cream, butter, and syrup. I move the sugar dispenser to make room for my coffee.

"Ominous much?" Darcy says.

"Austin's ex showed up when I was leaving to meet him for dinner."

Rosanna puts the syrup down. Darcy chokes on a mouthful of water.

"I think she had been waiting outside for a while," I add. "Like she knew where I lived and knew I was going to meet up with him."

Darcy waves her hands in front of her face frantically. Then she pops her eyes at me. "So. Many. Questions."

"What did she say?" Rosanna asks.

"She asked me why I was doing this. I told her that I didn't know Austin was married until the night I answered his phone and spoke to her. She said, 'I understand that, but why are you still with him?' The way she said it, it was like they were still together. There was no way I was going to remind her that Austin moved out and they're getting divorced. I didn't want it to blow up into this huge confrontation. So I said I had to go."

"You just left?" Rosanna says.

"What else was I supposed to do? I feel horrible about what happened. But like you guys keep telling me, their marriage falling apart wasn't my fault. I shouldn't have to defend myself to her." I take a pat of butter from the bowl and unwrap it. "This is one of the reasons I wasn't going to get back together with Austin. I don't want to have to deal with her. Does that make me a monster?"

"No," Darcy tells me. "It makes you human. Who wants to deal with their boyfriend's ex-wife?"

"Should I tell Austin about it?"

"You didn't tell him?"

"I felt bad for her, so I didn't say anything. I doubt she would tell him herself."

"But didn't you have dinner with Austin right after you saw her?" Rosanna asks. "How could you have pretended it didn't happen?"

"I don't know. I guess I just wanted to have one night without drama. The way it used to be. I mean, is this how it's going to be from now on? Where every time I see him, we're either talking about her or avoiding the topic?"

"Do you think you need more space?" Darcy asks. "If you and Austin take a break, she might chill."

"I've only seen him a few times since we got back together. Remember how I was telling you about his field study placement for the rest of the summer? He's not at my internship anymore." I cut off a small section of pancakes and drench it in syrup. I always like to have a few extra syrupy bites. But I have to limit the syrup drenching. Pouring too much syrup all over my pancakes makes me nauseous after I eat. Kind of like how talking about Austin's ex is making me feel now. "Whatever. Your turn, Rosanna."

"For what?"

"How's it going with Donovan?"

"Good." Rosanna stirs sugar into her coffee. "We've gotten a lot closer. I just wish . . ."

"What?" Darcy says.

Rosanna shakes her head. "No, I just . . . wish he wasn't hanging out with Shayla."

"That girl is still sniffing around?" Darcy scowls. "She needs to get a life."

"I don't think you have anything to worry about," I tell Rosanna in an attempt to take the sting off Darcy's bite. "It really seems like they're just friends."

Rosanna keeps stirring her coffee in slow circles, staring at her mug. "I didn't tell you guys this because I was trying to move on, but D and Shayla went out in high school. I had a feeling there was more to their history than just friendship. And I was right."

"See?" Darcy plunks down her coffee mug with emphasis. "What did I tell you? That girl has been trouble since day one."

"But that was a long time ago," I say. "You can be friends with someone after your relationship with them ends."

"Can you?" Darcy challenges. She points her fork at Rosanna. "Why don't you throw down an ultimatum? Either he stops hanging out with Shayla or you walk."

"He told me I don't have anything to worry about," Rosanna says. "Threatening him would be like saying I don't believe him."

"Do you?" Darcy asks.

"I'm trying to. Things are a lot better between us. Anyway, he doesn't even see her that much anymore. We've been together like every day." Rosanna smiles at Darcy. "But thanks for being so protective. You're a good friend."

"Any time."

"So what did you do last night?" I ask Darcy.

"Guess who I ran into at Lit Lounge."

"Who?"

"Remember that cute guy from Insomnia Cookies? The one at the counter I got shoved into?"

"The one who kept looking at you?"

"Yes! He was there. We talked for like two hours."

"Awesome! I knew he liked you!"

"Who is this?" Rosanna asks.

We tell her how we wandered around on Darcy's birthday, letting the energy of the city pull us in whichever directions it wanted. I was so excited that Darcy got the whole *look up* thing. She was totally into looking up and noticing beautiful details people don't usually see when they're walking around. And I loved that she loved those cookies. And that she captured my suburbanization rant on Bleecker Street. I posted the video a few days ago. So far there have been a decent number of views.

"What's his name?" Rosanna asks about the boy from Insomnia.

Darcy thinks for a second. "I don't remember. Blame it on one mojito too many. Or, um, three."

Rosanna and I exchange a look. Ever since Darcy found out Logan was scamming her, she's been drinking. A lot. Now that I know her credit card was confiscated and she found out about her dad's indiscretions at the same time she discovered the real reason Logan came here, I realize she's been trying to drown a lot more than just boy sorrows.

We're worried about Darcy. She's been covering up her drinking, playing it off like she's just tired or has a headache when we see her the next morning. But she's not fooling us. Rosanna even asked me if I thought we should do an intervention. Now might be a good time to ask Darcy how she's doing . . . and refuse to accept any answer besides the truth.

"We know this is an awful time for you," I begin, "but we just want to make sure you're okay."

"We?" Darcy says.

I gesture to Rosanna. "Us. Your roommates. The girls you live with. Who have noticed that you've had some pretty rough nights recently."

"The return of Summer Fun Darcy is reason to celebrate, not be concerned." Darcy picks at where her sparkly purple nail polish is starting to chip. "True, I might have been slightly on the hungover side this morning, but I rallied. End of story. Weren't we talking about boys?"

It's so Darcy to veer away from any subject she's uncomfortable discussing. But I follow her lead, because it might be the only way to talk to her.

"Are you seeing the boy from Insomnia again?" I ask Darcy.

"Yeah, no, he'll never call. That's what happens when you get too wasted and reveal too much."

"Like what?"

"Everything you're not supposed to talk about on a first date." Darcy laughs. "Like ex-boyfriends. Can you believe I talked about Logan *and* Jude? Not that it was a first date. It was more of a drive-by encounter."

"We like Jude," Rosanna chimes in.

"Who doesn't?" Darcy cuts a huge bite of pancakes, stuffing it into her mouth.

"I mean . . . we like him for you."

Rosanna and I exchange another look. We love Darcy and Jude together. I don't know what went wrong. One minute Rosanna and I are tracking Jude down at the park where he does his magic shows, explaining that we want him to fight for Darcy. The next minute Darcy doesn't want to talk about what happened when they got together at Dean & DeLuca. Whatever went down is wrong. And tragic. And, in my opinion, not too late to fix. But not until Darcy fixes herself.

"Jude officially wants nothing to do with me ever again," Darcy says.

"Are you sure?" Rosanna asks.

"He made it pretty clear when he walked out on me."

Darcy gives us a bright smile. "No worries. More boy adventures for me!"

"But he was just frustrated that you didn't know what you wanted," I say. Why is she playing this off like she wasn't hurt by Jude's rejection? "Everything's changed. You're not with Logan anymore. Does Jude know that Logan was trying to scam you?"

"Would it make a difference? I chose Logan over Jude. Even if Jude found out we're not together anymore, it would come off like he's a consolation prize if I say I want to get back together. That's not even—he wanted us to be exclusive. I can't promise him that."

I want to say: *Not like this. Not if you keep drinking to avoid your problems.* But now that Darcy is opening up, I can't press her. She's under enough stress already. And I don't want anything to come between us. Our Coffee Shop girl time means a lot to me. I would never forgive myself if we got in a fight. So I back off.

A threatening cloud has formed over our booth. This is not how I want us to remember Coffee Shop. I want us to be excited to come back here together, to know that this is a safe space where we support each other, not attack. The best way to be Darcy's friend in this moment is to support her the kindest way I can.

"Summer Fun Darcy is *back*!" I cheer.

Darcy's eyes brighten as she cracks a big smile. "She remembered what she came here for. She got distracted for a minute. But yes, she is back."

"Well if she's interested, the guy in 3A is looking for single girls. Not necessarily for him, although he is really cute. He's going to this party and needs a non-date."

"Sounds intriguing," Darcy says. "I'm in."

In a flash, I decide I won't reach out to Vienna about the party after all. The risk that Darcy would find out how I know Vienna is too high. That part of my life doesn't exist in this part.

We ping from topic to topic for what could be twenty minutes or two hours. Eventually Rosanna checks the time. "I hate to break up the fun, but it's almost one."

"No way," I marvel. "I thought it was like midnight. I can't believe how—" Then it registers. Rosanna checked the time on a cell phone. That she pulled out of her bag. And put on the table. "What. Is. That."

Darcy has been distracted by a waiter who looks like this actor I recognize from a show I can't remember. Now she looks over and sees the phone, too.

"Is that yours?!" Darcy shouts.

"D gave it to me last night," Rosanna says. "He just got the new version. He wasn't going to use it anymore and he found this cheap service for me, so . . ."

Darcy and I give each other an exploding pound.

"You have no idea how long we've been waiting for this day to come," Darcy tells Rosanna.

"We're really happy for you," I add. "Of course D just

got an even newer version of a phone I've been wanting forever."

"Tell me about it," Darcy says, admiring Rosanna's phone. "Can I just say how thankful I am that you finally joined this millennium?"

Rosanna is smiling, but Darcy and I seem way more excited about her phone than she does. "I know it will make life easier," she offers.

Darcy pulls out a wad of singles to pay. They must be her tips from working at the Place That Shall Not Be Named. She rolls her eyes at me. "Can you believe we have to keep up with *her* now? I can hardly afford pancakes, much less a new phone."

Rosanna giggles.

I'm happy that Darcy has a sense of humor about how the tables have turned.

We both are.

CHAPTER 8
DARCY

EVADING LOGAN WAS FUN AT first. Every time he contacted me, I blew him off. I wanted to see how long I could play him like he played me. But that game has become just one more annoying thing to maintain in Life After Daddy Destroyed Us. Maybe it's time to come right out and tell him I know. Only, where would the fun be in that?

Before my life morphed into a shape I don't even recognize, I was all fired up to annihilate Logan. But now I have a different perspective about what's important. Now my priorities are issues I never had to think about before.

Sadie was right. Logan doesn't deserve my energy. Or my attention. He doesn't even deserve to know that I know.

I'm still waiting to see how long it will take him to

come looking for me. So far it's been two weeks and four days. Doesn't he realize I'm avoiding him? Doesn't he care? Obviously not. He would know something was wrong if he really loved me. He would have come looking for me by now if he cared.

This could be part of his strategy. To wait and see when I'll come to him. He could have suspected I found out his nasty secrets. Or maybe he thinks I figured out he's been sneaking money from my wallet. Whatever is going on with him, it looks like he's going to lay low until I want to get together.

Screw that. I don't have time for that loser. If he wants me, he knows where to find me. Come and get it, scum-sucker.

My double shift ended half an hour ago when I closed. I wandered the streets aimlessly, wanting to get wasted but strangely unmotivated to find a cool bar with a hot guy to buy me drinks. Before I realized where I was going, I ended up here. In front of my dream apartment. I love standing in front of the big picture window, gazing in at the beautiful objects and absorbing the energy of this place. How can a home that belongs to someone else feel so much like my own? I don't even know who lives here. I've stood here like this a hundred times, wondering about the man on the other side of the glass. I've never seen anyone inside. But I have a feeling a guy lives here.

I take a few deep breaths, focusing on the Now.

Immersing myself in this moment. Allowing the soothing aura of this place I love to calm me.

A guy walks up to me on the sidewalk. I swiftly take in his classic American boy features—early twenties, brown eyes, brown hair, clean-cut—and deduce that he's not dangerous. He would be a more than acceptable candidate for my next boy adventure.

He peers in the window.

"Do you like it?" he asks me.

"This is my favorite apartment. I have to stop and drool every time I walk by. Not just because it's gorgeous. Something about it resonates with me."

"Would you like to come in?"

My mouth falls open. There is no way this is his place.

"It's my uncle's house," he explains. "I'm staying here while he's away on business."

WHAT. I actually have a chance to be on the other side of the glass?

The right thing to do is pass. I should thank him for the invite, say good-night, and move on. Girls aren't supposed to let boys they don't even know lure them into random apartments. But how is this any different from a one-night stand? I have gone home with boys I've only known for a few hours. Plus this isn't a random apartment. This place feels like home to me. Sadie would say that this boy inviting me in is a total non-coincidence. She would approve. We share a love of apartment stalking. I've told her how obsessed I am with this place. She will freak when she hears I got to go inside.

"I'm Tomer," he says.

"I'm Darcy."

"You can come in if you want. I promise I'm a nice guy. But no pressure."

I've always considered myself to be a good judge of character. Tomer does seem like a nice guy. Not only due to the lack of sketchy vibes. He has that same safe energy I feel when I look into his uncle's home.

"Thanks," I say. "That would be fantastic."

We climb the stairs to the front door. I can't believe this is happening. All the times I longed to be on the other side of the glass, I never thought I would actually get there.

Tomer pushes the door open, standing aside to let me pass. It's such a refined touch for a boy his age. Inside there's a hallway leading all the way back. To the left there is a staircase along the wall. Tomer puts his key in the lock of a door to our right.

A familiar connection intoxicates me the second I step inside the apartment. That same energy I felt when I was standing outside looking in is right here, all around me.

"This is unreal," I say. I go over to the big picture window I've gazed in so many times. I can almost see myself in the spot where I always stand outside. "I can't believe I'm on the other side of the glass."

"On the other side of the glass," Tomer repeats. He

comes over to look out with me. "Poetic."

Tomer shows me around. The apartment goes really far back. There's a huge kitchen behind the living room, followed by a dining room and a backyard garden. Tomer opens the glass door to the garden and turns on an outdoor light. There's another house across the garden.

"Do you know who lives there?" I ask.

"In the carriage house? My uncle owns that, too. He has some office space in there."

"What does your uncle *do*?" I blurt. As if I wasn't already acting like enough of a creeper.

"He's a music producer."

"Oh, cool."

"What about you?"

"My job is way less impressive."

"Are you in school?"

"Yeah, at UNY. I took summer session to make up some credits I missed while I was backpacking through Europe last year."

"That must have been amazing."

We sit at the kitchen counter and I tell Tomer all about my travels. He is fascinated. His questions surprise me. By what he's asking and his level of excitement, it seems like he's never been anywhere in Europe at all. I would assume this boy summered in Europe growing up. Everything about him screams he's from money. Watch Tomer turn out to be Donovan's cousin or something.

Tomer is so engrossed in the story I'm telling about this little artists' community in northern Italy called Bussana Vecchia that he has to snap himself out of it. "I'm sorry, can I get you a drink? I was going to have a beer."

"That sounds good." He takes two beer bottles out of the refrigerator. I watch him open them. Unless he found a way to open the bottles before I came in, slip any number of drugs into them, and seal the bottles back up so they still made that *fizz-pop* sound when he opened them again, they are safe to drink. I'm not worried about being in a strange boy's uncle's house anymore. And I'm definitely not worried about the consequences of getting drunk. Isn't that why I'm here? Isn't that why I'm staying? To numb the pain and forget about my life on the other side of the glass.

"Enough about me," I say. "Tell me something fascinating about you."

"I can play the harmonica and guitar at the same time."

"Really?"

"No. That's why I want to be Demetri Martin."

"Oh my god, I love him." Sadie showed me some of Demetri Martin's stand-up. He is hysterical without trying to be. Subtle humor everyone can relate to is the best. He did this whole thing about how cherry tomatoes in a salad are impossible to eat. They run away when you try to stab them with your fork and they burst juices at whoever is sitting across from you when you bite into them. So everyone avoids eating cherry tomatoes, which end up rolling around at the bottom of the bowl. So we should just agree to retire them from salads all together.

Tomer does some DM lines. "What's with those 'please use other door' signs on doors? You're a door. You're not a brick wall. All you have to do is open and close. Do your job."

"I love the large pad."

"Anything on the large pad. That dude has the best graphs."

"If math classes used Demetri Martin's graphs, math might actually be interesting."

"They would have to add those foot bells to make math interesting."

"So wait," I switch gears. "What's your story? How long are you staying here?"

"I'm starting grad school at Tufts. Just chilling here until the semester starts."

"What's your concentration?"

"Anthropology."

Wow. I didn't see that one coming. "What do you want to do with it?"

"Not sure yet. I'm leaning toward forensics, but journalism also has a hold on me. We'll see where the next two years take me." Tomer swigs his beer, then wipes his mouth with the back of his hand. "What about you?"

"I want to be a publicist."

"That sounds fun. I think you'd be really good at it."

"Why?"

"You seem like a social person. Don't PR reps have to be good with people?"

"They do."

"Well, I'm glad I got lucky with you." Tomer blushes at his double entendre. "Not—I meant that you're so nice and we're having a good time, not that . . . I'm just glad we met."

"Same." I give him a bright smile to let him know everything is okay. Tomer takes an awkward sip of beer, spilling some down his chin and wiping it away in a jagged motion. That's when I realize something surprising about him. Underneath the classic American boy features, he's kind of a dork. "I really appreciate you inviting me in. I still can't believe I'm here."

"This place is ridiculous." Tomer looks around the perfectly renovated kitchen with its marble counters, stainless steel appliances, and Sub-Zero refrigerator. "Can you imagine living like this?"

Now I'm confused. "Don't you? Live like this?"

"Are you kidding? My last apartment was gross. Four guys living in a cheap walk-up. It was a pit. The polar opposite of this place. My uncle has money, not me."

Tomer is not at all who he seems. I never would have guessed he's so down-to-earth. It's weird that I made all these assumptions about his life based on how he looks . . . and because he had access to my dream apartment.

How many people make assumptions about me based on how I look? What do they see when they look at me? A girl who appears to have her act together. A girl with style and expensive accessories. A girl who carries herself with confidence, who's not afraid to talk to people she doesn't know.

Underneath that cultivated exterior is a damaged girl whose world has been ripped apart. But she is determined to put it back together.

CHAPTER 9
ROSANNA

THE PROBLEM WITH PACKING ALL the clothes
Darcy gave me away in a bin is that now I have nothing
to wear.

It had to be done. I was an impostor wearing those
clothes. Who was I, thinking I could prance around New
York City in a wardrobe I could never afford?

I lost myself for a while. But now I'm remembering
who I am.

I am back with my ancient bunch of tattered clothes I
don't want to be seen in. Back to my ratty old skirts and
tops with holes from wearing them a million times and
outdated jeans that are practically illegal in New York. The
first time D saw me in my regular clothes, I was mortified.
He took me to dinner at Bocca di Bacco in Chelsea. The
least repulsive outfit I could slap together was a long black

skirt, a black top with a bit of shimmer, and my only black sandals. In theory the outfit should have worked. New Yorkers wear a lot of black when they go out. But I looked ridiculous. The skirt clung to my hips in the wrong places, the top was unflattering, and my sandals were clearly from a discount store. Walking to the restaurant, I kept catching reflections of myself in dark store windows, horrified by what I was seeing. I was almost in tears by the time I got there. D didn't say anything, though. He knows Darcy gave me those glamorous clothes and he knows I stopped wearing them. I guess he felt bad for me.

The way people on the street ignore me now that I'm dressed like a poor girl from the Midwest versus the impeccably polished girl I was in Darcy's clothes (except for my hair, which cannot be tamed) is like night and day. Guys flirted with me in those stylish clothes. Girls gave me appreciative smiles or seethed in jealousy. But now that I'm back to my old clothes, no one even looks at me. It's like I don't exist anymore. All because I'm not wearing the right things.

Before I moved here, I did not predict how well-dressed everyone would be. Even guys have a sense of style. They all have a look, like they've somehow figured out the best combination of clothing and accessories to reflect who they are. You can intuit a guy's personality just by catching a glimpse of him on the street.

Maybe if I actually knew who I was, or at least liked

myself more, I could figure out what my look should be. But I only know the person I want to be. I can visualize Shiny New Rosanna and I like what I see. I just have to keep moving forward until I am her.

I yank open another dresser drawer, hunting for a yellow shirt. I have yellow shorts that I got for like three bucks. Probably because they were yellow. Who wears yellow shorts? Besides me. I wear whatever I can find that's affordable.

D and I are doing an Improv Everywhere flash mob tonight. I signed up for their notifications after Mica told me about the group. Improv Everywhere sounded like the ultimate test to push myself to be more confident. What better way to conquer my fear of public attention than to participate in bizarre performances everyone will be staring at? This one is their annual Mp3 Experiment. The instructions said that each participant has to wear an all-over single color. We're also supposed to bring a balloon and a plastic shopping bag. They didn't say what for. Part of the fun is following directions along with everyone else in the moment. Not only are the observers surprised, but the participants are surprised, too. The only thing I know so far is that we have to meet down at Rockefeller Park before seven. The audio file will give us further instructions when we all hit play on our devices at 7:06 p.m. D giving me his old phone was perfect timing.

Yellow. I need more yellow. I could do a blue skirt and

tee, but I think there will be a lot of blue. Our rainbow shouldn't be askew because I gave up on yellow. Even though I'm not really into it, yellow is a happy sunshiny color, and therefore deserves equal representation.

There are no yellow tops in my dresser drawers. Looking in the closet would be a waste of time. I only have a few sad dresses hanging in there with a couple old jackets and a cheap winter coat that's never warm enough. Good winter coats are insanely expensive.

Sadie seems like a girl who would have lots of yellow. She is sunshiny bright. She might let me borrow a yellow top. I swing around to her room and knock on her open door. She's reading on her bed.

"Hey," she says. "Getting ready for the flash mob?"

"Yeah. Do you want to come with us?"

"It sounds like fun, but I'm in the mood for some self-empowerment." She holds up her book. The title is *Your Dream Life*. "Maybe next time?"

"Whenever you want." I have a peculiar impulse to flop on her bed like the girls on my shows are always doing with their friends. Partly because I've never had that kind of intimate friendship with any girl where I could just flop on her bed uninvited. Even when I went over to a friend's house and we hung out in her room back home, I either sat on the floor or perched uncomfortably at the foot of her bed.

Shiny New Rosanna could be a bed-flopper. But my

stubborn personality won't let her be free.

"We're supposed to wear everything the same color," I say. "Do you have a yellow top I could borrow? I could do blue, but—"

"Totally." Sadie gets up and goes over to her dresser. "What kind of top do you want?"

"Any kind would work."

She takes out a yellow tank top. Then a yellow tee. Followed by another yellow tank top.

"Take your pick," she says.

I smile at her three yellow tops.

"What?" she asks.

"Nothing." I pick up the first tank top she pulled out. "Thanks. I really appreciate it."

"No problem. You can borrow anything you want."

Slippery slope alert. Sadie has nice clothes. Not as designer as Darcy's. But they're cute. How would Darcy describe Sadie's style? Kind of girly boho with an urban edge. If I start borrowing Sadie's clothes, I would not be able to stop. Except for this one yellow time.

I yawn. We got home late from Coffee Shop last night. I didn't get to bed until after 1:30.

"I hear that," Sadie comments on my yawn. "I've been dragging all day. But in a good way. I love our Coffee Shop girl time. All our girl time."

"Me, too." It's amazing how close I feel to Sadie and Darcy. Sadie and I clicked right away over everything we have in common. Darcy and I got closer when I opened up to her. The friendships I had back home weren't like this. I had a few close friends, but it felt more like we were going through the motions. None of them felt like a real best friend.

I never thought I could be this close to anyone I met so recently, but here we are. I didn't expect to become so confident after seeing the way Sadie springs into action with her random acts of kindness. Now I'm also a person who takes action. I open deli doors for old ladies, run ahead on the sidewalk to pick something up that the person ahead of me dropped, throw a baby's tattered pink bunny to her mother through subway doors as they are closing. You can change in astounding ways when you allow yourself to become the person you want to be.

D meets me outside the Chambers Street subway station for the flash mob. He's all in red. Distressed red V-neck T-shirt, red jeans, and red Adidas high-tops.

"You look incredible," I say.

He kisses me. "So do you," he says. But I know I don't. Sadie's tank top and my shorts are way different shades of yellow. Neither of them fits right. My flip-flops are orange with yellow flowers. I didn't have any strictly yellow shoes.

"Not really," I mutter. "I had to borrow this shirt from Sadie. And I don't have any yellow shoes."

"We don't have to wear matching shoes."

"How do you know?"

"I watched videos of the other Mp3 Experiments. One of them had everyone dress in color blocks, but their shoes didn't matter."

"Oh." I should have found that video. That was stupid. "Should we head over?"

I nod, fumbling in my bag to see where my headphones are. I was rushing to leave so quickly I almost forgot them.

Tons of people are walking into the park. You can tell who the Improv Everywhere participants are by their colors. But usually the participants dress normally for flash mobs, making it impossible for observers to tell they're part of a group until they all play red light, green light on the sidewalk or something.

It's a little before seven. We look around at the other Improv players, commenting on the best outfits. A purple boy is wearing a purple tiara with huge purple feathers sprouting over his head. A red boy is wearing D's same sneakers. One green girl even painted her face green.

This is one group of New Yorkers I immediately feel comfortable with. They're not battling it out for five inches of lawn space at Bryant Park movie night or glaring at me at the Waverly Inn because I obviously don't belong there. Clearly, I have found my people.

I check the time. "It's seven-oh-three," I tell D. We take our phones out, plug our headphones in, and go to the Mp3 file we've downloaded. At exactly 7:06, we all hit play.

There's an "omnipotent narrator" named Steve. He will be giving us directions for the next forty-five minutes. The first thing Steve tells us to do is find people wearing our color. We have to divide up into our respective color blocks.

D makes a pouty face because we have to split up. I wave goodbye.

Yellows are hard to find. There aren't too many oranges, either. Just as I thought, a lot of people are wearing blue. Blue is the easiest color to pull off. All you have to do is wear a blue shirt with jeans. I find two more yellows and the three of us stick together, wandering bananas looking for the rest of our bunch. We eventually form a small yellow pond adjacent to the big blue sea.

Steve instructs us to take out the plastic shopping bag we were supposed to bring. We all do the wave with the bags on cue, raising them high in the air. There are so many people here I can't see beyond our group. I wanted to watch onlookers' reactions. A large red lake is on the side. I try to find D, but it's impossible. I wonder how many other reds are wearing red shoes. None of the yellows are wearing yellow shoes. I'm kicking myself for worrying over nothing.

Now we all take out our balloons. Steve tells us to blow them up and tie them. Then we keep our balloons in the air beach-ball style, tapping up any of them that come our way to keep them afloat. The colorful balloons bouncing above our blocks of color are making everyone smile.

The last thing we do is unplug our headphones and hold our devices over our heads. Ambient sounds chime through the air. We stand still like that for a few minutes, enjoying this moment of Zen on a sweet summer night.

"What did you think?" I ask D when I find him after.

"It was fun," he says. But his face tells a different story. He almost looks irritated.

"Are you okay?"

"Yeah. I just . . . thought there would be more to it."

"But you saw videos from the other years. You knew what to expect."

"No, it was cute. Did you have fun?"

"I loved it." Tonight was a perfect example of why I was dying to live here. Why I can't imagine living anywhere else. Why I feel like I've finally found my place to belong.

As we leave the park together, D reaches for my hand. I love walking around with him like this. I just wish we had the same level of enthusiasm when it comes to these kinds of activities. It took a while for D to start revealing his dorky side to me. He said he doesn't show it to just anyone. But D doesn't really seem that dorky to me. More like he knows a few dorky references. Anyway, dorky and weird are two different things. I don't think D will be into doing more Improv Everywhere events the same way I will. I wish he were as excited for the next event as I am. I wish this were something we could share.

We cross the street. "Wasn't that last part awesome?" I ask. "With the sounds?"

"What was that?"

"What do you mean?"

"What was it supposed to be?" D says. "What was the point?"

I can't believe he doesn't get it. "It was supposed to be awesome. It *was* awesome."

"Hmm. Guess I missed something."

Sometimes we truly connect. But other times he just doesn't get me.

CHAPTER 10
SADIE

AUSTIN PRESSES ME BACK AGAINST the couch cushions. He watches me in the candlelight.

"You're so beautiful," he says.

He kisses me again, over and over until it feels like we are the only ones here. The only ones in the whole world.

Rosanna told me about Otheroom after D took her here. It's a tiny bar with a tinier room in the back. Thursday is the most popular weeknight to go out, so I was stoked when Austin not only scored us space on the sectional sofa in the back room, but got us the corner spot. I've walked by this place on Perry Street a thousand times, but never thought about trying to get in. Kind of like when Darcy got us into that bar where Residue was playing. It just never occurred to me that I was finally old enough to try getting into bars I've walked by my whole life. Rosanna was right about it being romantic in here. The dimly lit room flickers with shadows cast by the light of candles scattered everywhere. Since it's so dark, you can make out all you want without people really noticing.

I want to stay here on this couch making out with Austin forever.

When Austin and I got back together, I told him I needed to take it slow. He reluctantly agreed to only seeing each other a few nights a week. I was trying to separate lust from love. But when we're alone together, especially in a place like this, lust takes over. When he kisses me, I remember how right we are together, how we fit together like puzzle pieces.

Austin slides his hand up my thigh. Too high. I put my hand on his to stop him. Dark corners of romantic bars can apparently be dangerous.

I reach over to the side table for my cherry soda.

"Sorry," Austin says. "You kind of drive me crazy."

"Only kind of?"

"No." Austin picks up his ginger beer and takes a sip. There's something super sexy about being in a dark bar with a cute boy drinking from a cold bottle on a hot summer night.

"How's it going at Trey's?" I ask. It must be strange for Austin to be living with a high school friend after being married.

"He's been great, but I really need to find a place."

"Was anything good listed today?" Austin has been looking for an apartment every day. He gets listings from a few different sources and goes to open houses for the ones that look okay.

"Yeah, if I want two roommates in Queens. I cannot believe how outrageous rents are. I read that New York City is now officially unaffordable to renters making minimum wage. In all five boroughs."

"So you might move back to New Jersey?"

"I don't have much of a choice." Austin traces his finger down my cheek. "Still think I can find that needle in a haystack?"

I remember our conversation over pie at Bubby's when I asked Austin why he lives in New Jersey instead of New York. He complained about the astronomical rents. I said that he could find the exception to the rule, an affordable place in lower Manhattan, if he looked hard enough. Like finding a needle in a haystack.

"This is New York," I say. "Anything is possible."

"Even getting back to the way we were?" The hopeful longing in Austin's eyes makes my heart flutter. I know, without a shred of doubt, that I will never stop loving this boy.

"I'm trying," I say.

"I never expected to be in a situation like this."

"Neither did I."

"You have a lot going on." Austin takes my hand,

squeezes it. "I don't want to add to your stress. I want to make you happy."

"You do."

"How's it going with Marnix being home?"

Just thinking about how to answer that makes this tiny back room feel less intimate and more claustrophobic. My history with Marnix is complicated. Way more complicated than a sister should feel about her brother. I don't want to talk about it, but I can talk about anything with Austin.

"I'm happy he's okay," I say. "And it's not like I'm still living at home, so . . ."

"What if you were?"

I drink some more cherry soda, trying to figure out how much to reveal. Austin used to be the person I could tell anything to. He was the only person I ever told about my sister. I felt like I could trust him with anything, which wasn't that long ago. He's the same person I knew before . . . or thought I knew before. Isn't he?

Austin waits patiently for my answer, open to whatever I want to share with him. This Stereophonics song "Rewind" comes on. I get caught up in his moody eyes, the flickering candlelight, and the nostalgic pull of the lyrics.

Don't waste your time
You can't make back

If you could rewind your time
Would you change your life?

Austin hasn't known me that long, but in a way he knows me better than anyone.

"Marnix scared me," I admit. "He would have these tantrums where he'd go ballistic. The smallest thing could set him off. One time when I was in tenth grade and he was a senior, he punched the wall next to my face so hard his fist went through the drywall. I ran to my room and blockaded the door. Marnix kept knocking on my door saying he was sorry. But I didn't let him in. The whole time I was sitting on the floor next to my bed, crying."

"That's intense."

I nod.

"Was that the only time he was violent?"

"There were a few other times he threw stuff. He smashed my mom's favorite vase when she wouldn't let him go to a party because he kept lying to her about doing his homework. But that's the only time I remember him almost hurting me. The crazy thing is, he wasn't even mad at me. He was yelling at my dad when he punched the wall. He didn't even notice I was standing there."

Austin rubs my arm to soothe me. It works. I feel better just having shared this with him. Everything will work out with Marnix. He is alive, which is the only thing that matters.

Flickering candlelight. Another song I love coming on. Austin's lips on mine. Everything else slips into the background.

I have no idea what time it is when we leave. And I do not care. The thing I love most about this summer is how I am free from time. In high school I couldn't just stay out all night doing whatever I wanted. I always had to race against the clock when I went out. Nights were never completely mine. Fun always had a predetermined expiration. No matter how much fun I was having, the deadline of my curfew was always there, bringing me down. My new freedom keeps astonishing me. I still can't believe I can stay out as late as I want, go wherever I want, do whatever I want . . . that this is my life now. I don't have to cram in epic experiences before the clock strikes nine. Those zings of panic I would get when I looked at the clock and saw I had ten minutes to make it home before my curfew have become a part of my history along with lockers and homeroom.

Time is now a key, not a lock. I am finally unlocking parts of living that were inaccessible before. Life can unfold around me the way it was meant to, naturally, without constraints. It's like my life has finally gotten to the good part where I can actually live it. Where I can just . . . be.

"Do you want to help me look for an apartment?" Austin asks when we're walking down Perry Street.

"Totally. But only if we can look for some here."

"Where? In the West Village?"

"Yeah. This is the best neighborhood."

"And the most expensive. You know I could never afford a place here."

"What about the needle in a haystack?"

Austin picks me up and holds me tight against him, my face right in front of his.

"You make me believe in magic," he says. "We'll look at a few places here."

"Really?"

"Really." He kisses me as people swirl around us. I hear one girl say how cute we are. The hum of traffic blends into other urban white noise I've heard my whole life. A dog barks. Crickets chirp. Way in the distance, a siren blares.

Even with these city sounds surrounding us, the rest of the world disappears again.

CHAPTER 11
DARCY

"WOULD YOU LIKE WHIPPED CREAM with that?"
I inquire of the grimy skater boy ordering an incongruous
frothy mocha concoction.

"No doubt," he confirms.

Ten years later when I've made his drink (extra time
accrued for having to redo the whole operation when I add
milk instead of heavy cream), I present it at the register,
complete with chocolate drizzle over the whipped cream.
He pays me. I'm about to count out his change when I see
who is standing in line.

Logan.

Took him long enough. Not that I want to see him.
But still.

Skater Boy is waiting for his change.

"Sorry." I snap into action, taking care of him and the

next two people in line. By the time it's Logan's turn, I still haven't figured out what I'm going to say. Or do. Throwing another drink in his face is an option. Bonus: I can make the drink extra sticky.

"I found you," Logan gloats. Like he hasn't known where I work. Like he didn't call me earlier today and find out I'm working a double.

"Here I am."

A middle-aged lady is in line behind Logan. She's tapping away on her phone. But her type-A vibe will probably only give me another minute to get rid of Logan before she gets impatient. "Working. Like I said."

"Can you take a break?"

The manager is restocking bags of ground coffee on the shelf above the machines. He looks over at us. My face must be showing how much I don't want to have this confrontation with Logan here because he says I can take my break early.

We go outside. We walk to Leroy Street and turn off busy Bleecker Street onto the empty block. A torrent of rage is swirling inside of me. I do not want to be near the place I work in case the torrent breaks out. Props for Sadie's protest and all, but my love life cannot become a spectacle.

"So what's the story?" Logan says, trying to keep up with me.

"With what?"

"You've been avoiding me."

"Have I?"

"Darcy." Logan stops walking. I stop with him. He hardly ever says my name. "What's going on?"

There is no point in evading the inevitable anymore.

"I know," I say.

"You know what?"

"Why you really came here."

"You wouldn't see me. I don't want to disrupt your work or whatever, but—"

"No. Why you came to New York."

"To get you back, babe." Logan reaches out to touch my arm.

"Stop it!" I shake him off. "Stop lying to me! I know you were trying to scam me out of money to pay off your bookie. I know about the money you stole from my wallet. I know about the girl you're seeing back home. I know everything."

Logan gapes at me. I can tell he is wavering between further denying and admitting the truth.

I wait to see which way he goes. If he keeps denying, I cannot be held responsible for any and all physical harm that may erupt on this loser.

He crosses his arms. "Where did you get all this?"

"From your email, where do you think?"

"You hacked into my email?" Logan says in a tone like this is the most egregious part.

"Um, no. I went to your laptop where your email was

open. Everything I needed to know was right there."

"It was still an invasion of privacy."

"What's worse: me invading your privacy or you lying to me this whole time?"

Logan drops the victim act. He has no weapon to fight this battle. "What do you want me to say?"

"What do you want to say?"

"I don't know."

I rip into him. "Because you didn't think you'd get caught? Did you really think I was going to fork over thousands of dollars for you to pay off some gambling debt?"

"I'm in trouble," he says so low I almost can't hear him. "I thought you'd want to help me."

"Help you? Help you play me even more? Help you dump me again when you get back home? So you can hook up with that bimbo? Are you insane?"

"She doesn't mean anything." Logan reaches for me again. I shake him off again. "She's nothing like you."

"Yeah. I think the problem is that I'm nothing like her. Is that it? I'm just not your type?"

"That's ridiculous. I love you."

"I don't think you do," I snap. "You wouldn't have been lying to me this whole time if you loved me." I blink back tears in spite of myself.

"I didn't want to tell you about the debt because I didn't want you to worry. And I swear she doesn't mean anything."

"Whose necklace was that?" I ask.

"What necklace?"

"The necklace I found under your bed the last time I spent the night."

"I don't—"

"Stop lying."

Logan glances down Leroy Street, hoping for someone to save him. But there is only me. The one who is ending us forever.

"Just tell me," I say.

"You said you didn't want to be exclusive."

"No, I said I wasn't going to see anyone else while you were here. I wanted to figure this out. I thought you wanted the same thing." I push down the Jude guilt that has surfaced without warning.

"I did."

"Then how did you think sleeping with some other girl would help us?"

"I didn't sleep with her. We hung out one night. That's all."

I knew it. I knew there was another girl. Turns out there were two other girls—the bimbo and the necklace.

Logan is doing his sexy sloucher thing with his dark hair tousling and his dark eyes smoldering. But the tousling and the smoldering no longer enchant me. I broke out from under his spell the day I woke up.

An old guy walking his little dog is shuffling toward

us. The comforting smell of freshly baked bread from the bread shop on the corner mocks me. A group of middle school girls shrieks with laughter as they stomp by on Bleecker Street. I refrain from screaming at Logan until the guy passes. The little dog's paws click on the sidewalk as they saunter past.

"So what you're saying," I venture, "is that you weren't just seeing one other girl. There were two. While I was entirely devoted to you? Did it ever occur to you that I could have been seeing someone else, but I chose not to? That I chose you over someone else I liked because you came all the way here to supposedly win me back?"

"You're the only one I love," Logan declares. His big eyes are desperate, pleading like a dog begging for table scraps. "Doesn't that matter?"

"No. Not when her necklace is under your bed and your hair smells like her lemon shampoo and the other one is sending naked photos of herself to you. Oh, and you're sending ones back." I am shaking with rage. "You are disgusting. I can't believe I fell for your bullshit again. But that has happened for the last time. We're done." I turn away and head back to work. I never want to see this scumbag again.

"Wait—"

"For what? More lies? I'm all set, thanks." I keep walking. I do not look back.

Logan doesn't follow me.

So that's it. We're over. I'm surprised our breakup wasn't more dramatic. When I found out Logan was scamming me, I was so furious I spent days avoiding him while I plotted the perfect revenge. Now I can't believe I was stupid enough to waste all that time thinking about him.

I take a minute to get myself together before going back into the coffee shop. I'm still shaking. I lean against a streetlamp, watching a steady stream of people flow by. How many of them have had their lives turned upside down? How many of them are heartbroken? How many are being deceived right now and don't even know it?

Sadie will understand my pain. Austin lied to her. She knows how it feels to have the person you love betray you. Except our situations are different. Austin loves Sadie. Logan doesn't love me. He probably never did. He ended up breaking my heart twice. But now I know that wouldn't have happened if he'd truly loved me from the start. Which is why Sadie would encourage me to never give up on my search for true love. If she were here, she would tell me that my soul mate could be right around the corner. She would remind me that anything is possible in New York. She would point to the epic non-coincidence of last night as an example. How else would I explain the timing? That Tomer just happened to be staying at his uncle's place? That he came home right when I was standing there?

I knew Tomer was a nice guy. He didn't push me to drink. He didn't try to take advantage of me. I considered getting sloppy drunk to bring on the numb, but I didn't need to be numb with Tomer. We had the best time just talking.

And then there's Jude. . . .

Sadie is right. Anything is possible.

When I feel ready to take control of my life, I take a deep breath in front of the coffee shop. Then I open the door.

CHAPTER 12
ROSANNA

THE APARTMENT IS SO QUIET, all I can hear is the hum of the air conditioner. When I first moved here, the traffic noises out on 5th Avenue kept me awake at night. I don't even notice them anymore. The traffic has blended into the background noise. I actually like how it's never completely quiet here. City noises remind me that there is always something going on right outside my door. The constant activity makes me feel less alone, even when I'm feeling extra lonely like tonight.

I lie on my bed looking around my room. D is working late tonight. Same with Darcy. Sadie is at Otheroom with Austin. She must be loving it. As soon as D took me there and I saw all that candlelight, I knew it was a Sadie place.

I'm not as homesick as I was when I first moved here. But there are times when I think about my family and feel so far away. We talk all the time, but it's not the same as being with them in person. Not at all.

A picture from my eighteenth birthday party sits on my dresser. My friend's parents own a pizza place and they let me have my birthday party there for free. The picture is of me and four friends standing around a table. My mom baked a cake that day, and I caught her tearing up when I went into the kitchen while she was mixing the ingredients. She couldn't use her onions excuse for why her eyes were watery. She told me she was emotional about baking my last birthday cake while I was living at home. Since my birthday is in early December, I'll be at college for my birthday from now on. And then in grad school. And then being a social worker, hopefully here in New York. She was probably baking my last mom-baked birthday cake ever.

I push myself up from my bed and go over to my dresser, picking up the picture frame. Every time I look at this picture it bothers me that I didn't stand up straight. I'm standing in the middle of my friends, kind of hunched over. They are all standing up straight with pretty smiles. I should have smiled in that picture as brightly as they did. If only my posture had been better, I'd be looking at this picture with fond memories instead of kicking myself. Why can't I embrace being tall instead of feeling so self-conscious? Regretting everything I should have done in pictures is not the way I want to live my life. I need to accept my height for what it is. I need to quit fighting the parts of me I don't like but cannot change.

Out of the corner of my eye, I detect someone at a window across the alleyway. Not just any window. His window.

We got lucky with our apartment. Some other apartments have windows that look out on air shafts. They have no views or light. My windows face another building, but it's far enough away to offer some privacy and let light come into my room; plus I'm close enough to the corner to see part of 5th Avenue to the right. The other day I was looking at some of those windows I could see into, wondering who lived in each apartment and where they came from, when a boy suddenly appeared in a window one floor above mine. From what I could tell he was around my age. He looked cute. There was a UNY cap on his windowsill along with a baseball in a clear display cube and a struggling philodendron, half-wilted with too many yellow leaves. He just came right up to the window eating a piece of toast, looking out toward 5th Avenue. And there I was, one floor below him, staring right into his apartment.

I lurched away from the window, stubbing my toe on the bed frame and nearly taking out a lamp, showing off my ineptitude at covering up overt spying.

I didn't think the boy eating toast saw me. But now he's back in the window. Just standing there.

Looking right at me.

My first instinct is to bolt. When it comes to fight or flight, I am all about the flight. But I want to be more confident. This could be a test to see how much I want to fight for it.

I peek up at him.

He smiles at me.

I smile back.

He waves.

I wave back. My heart is doing jumping jacks.

He moves away from the window. Did I do something wrong? Was my wave weird? I am still as a statue, waiting to see if he will come back.

Hoping that he will come back.

Why am I hoping? Why it is so exciting to be sort of flirting with a boy in a window? Should I even be doing this when I have a boyfriend? What would D say if he found out? But as long as nothing happens, I think it's harmless.

The boy comes back. My heart breaks out in a riot of jumping jacks.

He holds a sign up against the window for me. HI is written in black marker on plain white paper.

Now what? Should I write something back?

Only if I want to be Shiny New Rosanna. Which I do.

I grab a Sharpie from my desk and some paper from my printer. This ancient printer will deserve a trophy if it makes it through all four years of college.

I write HI back. Original, I know. My jumping-jack heart is making it impossible to be more creative.

He sees my HI and raises me an I'M BRANDON.

Do I have to give him my name? Would it be a security risk if I did? Not that he could track me down from only a first name. But he already knows where I live. He could easily find out that my building is UNY student housing. If he searched the student directory for girls with my first name, I would quickly come up. How many Rosannas can there be at UNY?

But then what? What do I really think this guy would do if he knew my last name? Be all twisted like Addison and make my life a living hell? Darcy has been trying to get me to come out of my shell. Like I'm a turtle instead of a girl lacking self-esteem. Maybe she's right. Maybe if I were more like Darcy, I wouldn't be worrying about the boy next door's secret identity as a serial killer. Darcy's priority is to have fun. When has my priority ever been to have fun? Never. I could try it now, just for one night. Just to see what happens.

I make a new sign and hold it against my window. I'M ROSANNA.

Brandon writes on a new piece of paper. My jumping-jack heart refuses to slow down.

His new sign says CALL ME? With his number.

Okay. This just got real.

Too real for me.

I can't call a random boy who knows where I live. What would I even say? That I already have a boyfriend, but thanks for the interest? That would only irritate him and make him more likely to lash out against me. Especially if he is a serial killer.

On the other hand, I don't want to completely shut him down. That would hurt his feelings. So I take a fresh sheet of paper and write SORRY, I HAVE A BOYFRIEND. I hold it up to the window, trying for an apologetic expression to go along with breaking the news.

He shrugs and smiles. Then he does a little salute thing before he disappears farther into his apartment.

I really should be more careful about keeping my blinds closed. But I like having them open. I like how sunlight shifts the mood of my room throughout the day. At night, I like being able to see the city lights and other people's lit windows. It calms me to see that there are lots of people around me in their homes, living their lives in the same space as mine.

Now it's going to be awkward. Whenever I have my blinds open, I'll be wondering if he's looking in. Or I'll be looking into his apartment to see if he's there. What if I see him on the street? Would he recognize me? He could be one of those coffee shop guys always on their laptops where Darcy works. Or he could show up in one of my classes when fall semester starts. The boy could be anywhere.

I think about all these scenarios again later as I try to fall asleep. Not because I want to meet him. That would be embarrassing. I have no idea what he's seen me doing in my room. Or what he's seen D and me doing in my room. It's more like I am letting my mind drift over all the possibilities of people interacting in this city. We affect one another every day in ways we don't even realize. An incredible amount of potential exists for us to help one another, for us to reach out and show other people that we are all in this together. No matter what we are all going through, chances are at least one other person here is dealing with the same thing.

I must have drifted off to sleep without realizing it because a scratching sound jolts me awake. Normal night sounds are Darcy coming home or Sadie going to the bathroom. This is not a normal night sound. And it sounds like it's coming from inside my room.

*Scritch-scritch-scritch. Taptaptap*tap!

Adrenaline sears my veins. There is something in the corner by my dresser.

I don't want to know what it is.

I have to know what it is.

I reach over to the lamp on my nightstand and turn it on. The noise stops. Then I see a gray blur streaking along the baseboards to my door.

A mouse. The gray blur is a mouse.

I scream. I don't know who else is home and I feel bad

about waking anyone up. But I can't help it.

Sadie rushes to my room.

"What's wrong?" she asks.

"Don't stand on the floor! There's a mouse!"

Sadie yelps. She leaps up on the foot of my bed.

Darcy appears in the doorway. She doesn't seem like she knows she's awake.

"Are you guys okay?" Darcy says.

"No, we are *not* okay," Sadie huffs. "There's a mouse."

"It went that way." I point to the living room.

"A mouse?" Darcy is slowly waking up.

"Yes," I confirm.

"In our apartment?"

"I saw it."

Darcy absorbs this information. I can't believe she wasn't smacked into consciousness as soon as she heard the word *mouse*. She does not look anywhere near as panicked as me or Sadie. Darcy stands strong, hands on hips, giving us a terse nod.

"That fucker is going down," she intones.

We gape at her.

She strides out to the living room like a mouse didn't dash that same way a minute ago. Sadie and I scream.

"Oh, relax," Darcy mumbles. She comes back to my room with the broom.

"What are you going to do?" Sadie trills, hopping from foot to foot on my bed.

"I'm going to show that intruder who's boss!" Darcy booms. "Some mouse thinks he can dance around this place like he runs the joint? I don't think so."

We gape at her some more. I can't believe Darcy is so in control of this situation. So not afraid. I know Sadie is thinking the same thing.

"You said it went into the living room?" Darcy asks us. We nod.

"Sit tight," she says, wielding the broom. "I'll go investigate." She takes off into the living room like Wonder Woman. Lights start coming on in the living room and kitchen.

"Wow," I breathe.

"Who was that?" Sadie breathes back.

"Did you see how unfazed she was?"

"I know. How is she not freaking out right now?"

There is no way I'm going back to sleep. Even if Darcy smashes that mouse to smithereens like she did with the smoke detector.

"Have you ever had mice before?" I ask Sadie.

"Not as a regular thing. But some of my friends had them. Wildlife kind of comes with the West Village territory. I am just not a fan of indoor wildlife."

"What if there's more than one?"

"Ooooh!" Sadie does her hopping thing again. "Don't say that! I have to get back on the floor to go back to my room."

"But we have the lights on."

"Doesn't matter. My friend Heather kept her light on all night and she still had a mouse in her room. Or mice. Gross!"

I sit up higher, throwing my light blanket and sheet off. I'm drenched in nervous sweat.

"We have to put traps down," Sadie strategizes. "Glue traps. The big ones." She cranes her neck toward my doorway, trying to see what Darcy is doing. Banging noises are coming from the kitchen. "I cannot believe this is happening. Jesse said the building was fumigated. He said I didn't have to worry."

"Who's Jesse?"

"That cute guy in 3A."

"Oh yeah. Can't the exterminator do our apartment?"

"Totally. I'll look into that."

"You think you're smarter than me?" Darcy bellows from the kitchen. "Watch who's smarter when I move this stove, bitch!"

It's official. Darcy Stewart is my hero.

"Should we go help her?" I ask, secretly hoping Sadie will say no.

"Um. It sounds like she's got it under control."

"How can one little mouse be so loud?" I wonder. "It was making this tapping noise like it kept scraping something against the floor."

"Where was it again?"

I point to the corner by my dresser.

Sadie looks over. "It might have been chewing on the lamp cord. Or maybe something fell behind your dresser?"

Darcy comes back, waving a frying pan. "I figured out how it got in. There's a hole in the wall behind the stove."

"You moved the stove by yourself?" I ask.

"It's a cheap stove. It slides out, no problem."

"We have steel wool," Sadie says. "In the utility closet. We can plug the hole with that."

"Did you find any other holes?" I ask.

"Not yet. But the coast is clear if you guys want to come look."

"Except we don't know where it came from," Sadie warns. "There could be another hole somewhere else."

"Why do you think I have this?" Darcy holds up the frying pan. "I will flatten any mouse who dares come in here again."

"I'll call the super in the morning," Sadie says.

There is no way I'm going back to sleep. I will be wide awake until the super gets here. So I might as well help Darcy look. I swing one leg over the side of the bed.

"What are you doing?!" Sadie panics.

"We should help Darcy."

"But that would require walking on the floor."

"Don't worry. She's protecting us." I get out of bed and reach a hand up to help Sadie down. "You can do this."

Sadie tentatively climbs down on shaky legs.

Am I really more confident than Sadie right now? I can't believe I'm the one helping her instead of the other way around.

We creep out to the kitchen. Darcy has every light in the apartment blazing. Sadie stuffs steel wool into the hole behind the stove. Darcy hands us flashlights, splitting us up into areas like we're detectives combing a site for clues.

If Brandon were watching us, I wonder what he would think. Would he assume we're just three roommates looking for a mouse? Or would he be able to tell that, against all odds, we are so much more?

CHAPTER 13
SADIE

ONE THING I LOVE ABOUT skyscrapers is that they didn't exist before. Before each skyscraper was there, there was only empty space in the sky. Someone contemplated the potential of that empty space. They conjured a magnificent structure out of thin air. Then they manifested their vision by constructing an entire building. They created something from nothing. They turned their dream into reality.

New York by Gehry is one of those striking skyscrapers that gives me chills every time I see it. Its twisty, undulating shape and hard metallic luster make it stand out as an architectural gem. There's no other skyscraper like it. I love it best in this light, all glowy brilliance before sunset, illuminating its unique curves. Slick and sophisticated. Radiant and beautiful. Making me feel like any dream can become reality, including dreams as big as this one.

Every architect who looked up into nothing and imagined it into something believed the impossible was possible. The New York City skyline exists because of them. And we can see the entire history of our skyline right here at the Skyscraper Museum.

"This one's so weird," Darcy says. She leans closer to the sketch of Central Park Tower. "It looks like a pencil. How can buildings even be this skinny? This one looks like a strong wind would snap it in two."

I read the information card next to the sketch. When Central Park Tower is completed, it will be the tallest residential building in the world. The developer said it will be one foot shorter than One World Trade, the building that stands next to where the Twin Towers once stood, out of respect. Now I like this building even more.

"I think it's cool," I say. "And I'm pretty sure it won't have an indoor wildlife problem."

Darcy crashed last night around four, but Rosanna and I were too wired from mouse trauma to sleep. We stayed up all night talking in my bed with the lights on. Rosanna propped the broom against my nightstand in case the mouse or any of its associates decided to make an encore appearance. I called the super at nine on the dot. Luckily he came right over.

"But this building was fumigated," I protested as the super worked in the kitchen. He filled every hole and gap we discovered last night with foam. He also put down traps. I don't know which is scarier: a mouse running around our apartment or a mouse caught in one of the traps, squealing in agony or chewing its leg off. "Why are there still mice?"

The super did a loud tooth suck. "Even monthly exterminations don't solve the problem completely. I'll add you to the list."

Last night was a night of extremes. I went from the rapture of making out at Otheroom with Austin to the terror of encountering indoor wildlife. My head is still spinning from the brutal 180.

Darcy and I advance to the next room of the museum. A One World Trade Center retrospective covers an entire wall. We face a huge photo of the Twin Towers taken after their opening in 1973. It's hard to believe that two buildings so tall and majestic could be destroyed. That when we look toward the holes they left behind in the sky, people were once seeing those towers there. This is why One World Trade is my favorite building. It represents what is possible in the impossible. It represents hope and freedom. Rosanna and I have been talking about good winning over evil, and I think One World Trade is the embodiment of that mighty force. The fact that this building is standing today shows how we can be triumphant in the face of adversity, no matter how horrible the circumstances.

Darcy looks at me. "Do you remember September Eleventh?"

"No, I was too little. But Marnix remembers some of it. It was like his second or third day of school when it happened. He didn't know what was going on. No one did."

We read more World Trade Center history. The last part of the retrospective is about One World Observatory, the observation deck on top of One World Trade.

"We should go there with Rosanna," I say.

"Definitely." Darcy yawns.

"I think this is the first time I've ever seen you yawn."

"Staying up all night with a hot guy is a lot different than staying up all night hunting a mouse. Or it could be my job. Satisfying coffee addicts' designer-drink demands is not as easy as I thought it would be. All it takes is one double shift to wear you down."

"How did you get tonight off?" I ask as we move to the next room.

"I switched with someone else. Jude called me this morning. He wants to get together tonight."

I screech to a stop so suddenly the lady behind us bumps into me.

"Sorry!" I apologize.

She walks on in a daze as if we never collided.

"You waited all this time to tell me?" I ask Darcy, incredulous.

"I'm trying not to get my hopes up. He could just want to be friends. Or he could just want to tell me how horrible I am to my face."

"Dude. This is karma. How else can you explain the timing? Jude calls you the day after you break up with Logan? That's a non-coincidence. The Universe is balancing out the BBB."

"The what?"

"Bad Boy Behavior. Logan was such a dumbass. Now you're getting what you deserve." I bust out a dorky happy dance right here in the middle of the Skyscraper Museum. "We love Jude. And we love Jude for you."

"We?"

"Rosanna and I. We discussed the situation and concluded that you guys should be together. Go, karma!"

Darcy sits on a bench. I sit next to her, still a little jumpy as my dorky happy dance winds down.

"I'm not sure karma works that way," Darcy says. "Balancing everything out."

"Not everything. Just parts of your life that have been extreme."

"But just because someone is getting badness thrown at them doesn't mean goodness is going to rush in and even everything out."

"No, I just think that if you're a good person, which you are, karma works with the positive energy you put out into the world. It's like this power that helps a part of your life get better when things keep going wrong."

"Not always," Darcy argues. "Take my mom. My dad has been cheating on her for years. Did karma swoop in and balance things out? No. He destroyed their life together and left her with nothing."

"But that could have been karma."

Darcy looks at me like I'm crazy. "I thought karma was supposed to be a good thing."

"It is! I mean, I am so sorry about what's happening to your mom, but in the long run this could be a good thing for her. Do you really want her to stay with your dad? After everything he's done?"

"You're saying you think she's better off without him?"

This is tricky. I totally think she's better off without him. Hello, he's a cheater and a liar. But of course I can't tell Darcy that.

"Do you?" I ask, hitting the ball back into Darcy's court.

Darcy is quiet for a minute. "Sometimes things have to get worse before they can get better," she says. "Maybe that's happening to me. Do you think Jude wants to get back together?"

"I hope so."

"Damn."

"What?"

"I didn't want to get my hopes up. Now my hopes are up."

"What did he say?"

"Only that he wanted to show me something. He gave me an address. I'm supposed to meet him there at eight."

"Maybe he moved."

"Or maybe it's his new supermodel girlfriend's place and he wants to show her off."

I take some supershine lip gloss out of my bag. Lip gloss is so much easier to find in the small bags I carry now. Why did I ever feel the need to lug so much stuff around?

"Want some?" I offer the tub to Darcy.

She takes a little, delicately dabbing it on over her bright pink lipstick. Now I know why she looks extra glam tonight. She is always polished, but tonight she's wearing a slinky aqua bodycon dress with the peacock espadrilles I love. She is shimmering like an ocean.

"You look amazing," I tell her. "Sexier than any supermodel. Trust me, you have nothing to worry about."

"Except what Jude wants."

"What if he does want to get back together? Do you want to be in a relationship?"

Darcy adjusts the strap of her dress. "All I know is I want him in my life."

"He obviously feels the same way. If he didn't want you in his life, he wouldn't have called."

"There you go getting my hopes up again."

"Hope is a good thing," I say. "Always."

We leave a few minutes later so Darcy can go to Jude's mystery address and I can go home to work on warm fuzzies. My high school friends and I are having a Last Blast party on August 19 before most of them go away to college.

I've been making warm fuzzies for all of them. The warm fuzzies will look cute on their bulletin boards. They are kind of my way of sending a piece of me with them.

"Go, karma," I repeat out front.

Darcy gives me a wistful smile. "I hate that bad things happen to good people. It would be so much easier if bad things only happened to bad people."

She's right. Karma isn't simple. But even with its complications, I can never stop believing that good will prevail.

CHAPTER 14

DARCY

I'M NOT READY TO RING the bell.

As long as I stay outside the building Jude told me to meet him at, I can bask in the light of that auspicious flame Sadie stoked at the museum. The hope that Jude wants me back in his life is like radiant sunshine. Here outside the front door, I can be the optimistic girl Sadie wants me to be.

But what if he does want me back? As a girlfriend?

When Sadie asked me if I wanted to be in a relationship, not exclusive casual but committed all the way, I didn't know how to answer her. With any other boy, I would say no. This city is *en fuego* with hotties. But everything changes when it comes to Jude. He makes my stomach flip, my heart flutter, and my protective layer fall apart.

Reality comes crashing in as a high school boy on a

skateboard zips by, nailing a jumping trick that sends him flying off the curb. Being fooled by Logan. My dad destroying our family. All the relationships that have crashed and burned around me over the years. Someone always gets hurt.

I know how painful it is to be the someone who gets hurt. But I have been that someone for the last time.

I ring the bell. The door buzzes after a few seconds. I push it open and step inside the mystery building. There's a small lobby tastefully decorated with an entryway table, a mirror, and a palm tree to the right. Two rows of mailboxes are centered on the left. An elevator waits at the far wall to take me to wherever I am meeting Jude.

Suite 200 doesn't have a sign on the door, so I still have no clue where I am. I see a doorbell and speaker on the wall, but the door opens before I can ring the bell.

Jude is standing right in front of me like it's totally normal for him to be opening a door where I'm on the other side.

"You found me," he says.

Every cell in my body vibrates. I take a deep breath, forcing what I hope comes across as a relaxed smile. "After some serious navigation. Could the Financial District be any more confusing?"

"Well I'm happy you're here. Step into my office."

I brush past Jude, worrying that I'm too sweaty for my

Vera Wang Princess to be working its charms. Damn you, August.

Jude closes the door. We just stand there for a minute, smiling at each other. He looks good. Scary good. So scary good I'm terrified I might make a huge mistake and beg him to take me back. Jude is rocking board shorts in sunset colors with a palm tree on the side, a threadbare tee in a vibrant shade of blue that makes his eyes pop, checkered Vans, and a glowing tan. His blue eyes glitter. His blond hair has more highlights from being out in the sun than the last time I saw him.

Oh yeah. The last time I saw him. When Jude said he wanted to fight for me, but he didn't know what he was fighting for. The problem was, I didn't know, either.

A ball bouncing on the hardwood floor somewhere inside alerts me that we are not alone. I look around and see that this is a huge, open-concept office with desks set up in clumps. Apparently Jude's startup is a hit. A big conference table sits in the middle of everything, next to a wall of windows. I follow Jude farther in and discover another desk clump in a corner. A guy is bouncing a basketball in front of a hoop hanging from the wall.

"You ever gonna take a shot?" another guy sitting at his desk asks.

"That's Harrison with the ball," Jude tells me. "And that's Dax at the desk. They're my tech geniuses."

Dax swivels around in his chair, his hands clasped behind his head, leaning back. He grins at Jude. "Can you tell your minion playtime is over? We're only half-done with configuring the software update."

"I'm in the zone." Harrison frowns. "You know this is how I boost creative flow." He sits down at the desk across from Dax, clearly bummed. The basketball gets dropped into his bottom desk drawer. His desk is impressively neat for a dude. Folders are color coded in even stacks. Clear acrylic desk organizers in a variety of shapes and sizes hold everything from pens to rubber bands to staples. Even his laptop is centered exactly in front of his chair. Dax's desk is a sharp contrast. Papers, books, and random tech gear are splayed everywhere. Mounds of paper clips are scattered around. Harassed Post-its are stuck to everything. Detritus is sprinkled over the top of his mess like Romano on pasta.

"Hey, Jude," Dax says. "Can we still submit those dinner receipts from last week?"

Jude nods. "You can be reimbursed for any dinner you have here after nine."

Dax rummages through some crumpled receipts. "They're here somewhere," he mumbles.

"Good luck with that," Harrison snarks. "Can we please get back to work?"

"Oh, now you want to work. What happened to elevating creative chi or whatever?"

"Boosting creative flow."

"Let's hit it." Dax snaps his focus to his laptop, clicking away on the keys so fast I linger there watching for a minute. Along with Dax and Harrison, two other people are working late.

This is the kind of office where you see windows lit up all night. It's so *How to Make It in America*. I loved that show something fierce, and not just because Bryan Greenberg is a delicious slice of man. Bryan's character starts a line of jeans called Crisp. He has a business partner, and they keep trying out different start-up ideas. They are on the grind 24/7. Always hustling and networking and doing every single thing they can think of to succeed. Not just succeed. They want to be grassroots rock stars. Failure is not an option for them. Their determination to become zillionaire entrepreneurs reminds me of Jude. You can feel that same energy here in his office.

Jude tells me about his seven employees. He has Dax and Harrison doing tech, two creative developers, one administrative assistant, one accountant, and one social media expert. That thing where everyone is constantly bursting into creative flame is infectious. It makes me want to figure out a name for my PR company and design a logo when I get home tonight.

"He'll never find those receipts," Jude whispers to me as we walk past the conference table to the other end of the open office space.

"You think?"

"Harrison submits his receipts like two seconds after he finishes eating. I was hoping his organization skills would rub off on Dax. Still waiting on that."

"Did they know each other before they started working here?"

"Yeah. They moved over together from a big coding firm where they were cogs in a machine. How could you tell?"

"I don't know. It was just a feeling I had."

Jude smiles at me. "You really are good at reading people." He leads me to a cozy corner with a lime-green couch, little round ottomans with aqua and lime stripes, and a round glass coffee table. "This is me."

For a crazy second I think he means this corner of the office is where he lives. Then I see his desk next to the window. Jude's desk is not as neat as Harrison's or as messy as Dax's. It's somewhere in between.

"This is so cute." I sit down on the couch, testing it out. "Puffy but firm. I like it."

"I never realized how many couches looked good but felt like you were sitting on a rock until I was looking for one."

"Good choice of colors." I pat an aqua throw pillow. "Any cozy couch corner that matches my outfit is winning."

Jude sits next to me. But not so our legs are touching.

He is just out of reach.

I look around the office. "This is amazing. I'm really proud of you."

"Thanks."

"Do you usually work this late?"

"Yeah. Working insane hours is typical for start-ups. I get in around ten and work until one or two."

"One or two in the morning?"

"Yep."

"When do you sleep?"

"What's that?" Jude laughs. "The hours are crazy, but they're worth it. This will all pay off when companies start buying my products. I'm working on thirty-two different patents now."

"Whoa! What are they?"

"A bunch of homelife improvements. You know, tweaks to make your routines run more smoothly. We're marketing them like little bits of everyday magic. Remember how I told you about those spray and pump bottles that guarantee usage of the entire contents? My investors wanted to brand all my inventions in a coherent way. So I thought of some other things I could develop. Like a vacuum sealer clip for cereal to keep it fresh."

"Don't they already have those air-tight cereal containers?"

"Yeah, but how many people actually use those?"

"No one I know."

"Exactly. It's much easier to keep your cereal in their original boxes, which is what most people do. This clip allows the bag inside the cereal box to act just like those cereal containers."

"How did you think of that?" I am zapped by a jolt of inadequacy. I cross my legs, smoothing my dress over my lap. Jude is this brilliant inventor and what am I?

Jude stretches his arm out along the top of the couch cushion. Kind of like he's putting his arm around me without touching. "Anyone can think of this stuff. I just have too much free time. Had."

"So I guess you haven't been doing a lot of shows."

"I'm taking a hiatus. But I'll get back to the other magic when things settle down."

Jude loves performing magic for his enthusiastic crowds. Making people happy makes him happy. But I wonder if he really will go back to that part of his life. The way his company is taking off, it would be sort of weird for Jude to want his Before life back. Scraping by and living with three other guys in a crappy apartment doesn't sound like good times.

"Do you still live on Spring Street?" I ask.

"For now. But I'm looking for a new place."

"So is Austin."

"Who?"

"Sadie's boyfriend."

"Oh yeah."

An awkward silence settles over us. I recross my legs, looking around some more. This really is a cute space. Kind of hipster industrial with some wall sections covered in chalkboard paint, a tall tree in front of the windows, and high ceilings with red heating and cooling tubes showing. The exposed brick along the long wall with windows is painted a glossy white. The windows are tall, with charming arches and wide windowsills where cheerful plants are gathered. The hardwood floors gleam.

A police siren down on the street breaks the silence, gradually amplifying as it passes the building, then fading out.

Jude clears his throat. "Sorry—do you want something to drink?"

"No, I'm okay."

"Because I'm the kind of boss who keeps quite an assortment of beverages in the fridge."

"You have a kitchen?"

"Over here." I follow Jude to the area of the office closest to the front door. A lounge with a smattering of tables, chairs, and benches is arranged next to a corner kitchen. Jumbles of papers, folders, pens, markers, and gadgets are piled on the tables and benches. Abandoned coffee cups are all over a table. I imagine Jude and his creative team meeting there, design ideas sparking as they chug cup after cup of coffee, getting so revved up with inspiration that they fly to their desks without bothering to clear the table. A powder-pink cardigan is draped over the back of a chair. A laptop sleeps on another table. There's this lingering electricity in the air that was generated when Jude's people were sitting here before. I can almost feel the residual heat from the crackling fire of his team tapping away at their laptops, plans unfolding faster than anyone can record them, everyone on their phones. This is what I love most about New York City: the intensity, the drive, the passion. The energy is like a drug I live on.

Jude is addicted to the same drug. You have to be to create all this. Jude Bryant is a nineteen-year-old self-made entrepreneur whose rich parents did not help him at all. He is a rock star. And he's only just begun to shine.

It would be hilarious if I ended up being Jude's publicist.

Even more hilarious is how both of our lives have been completely transformed since we met. Jude's life has become tremendously better while mine couldn't get much worse. But Jude's life didn't improve on its own. Jude is the one who made this happen. Scoring those major investors. Obtaining enough funding to pay the rent on this office and salaries for seven employees. Working on thirty-two patents. Everything Jude has he created. He changed his life by taking action.

Jude took control of his life and turned it around. I hope I'm doing the same with mine.

"Are you sure you don't want a drink?" Jude asks. He

opens the refrigerator's clear glass door to an entire top shelf crammed with bottles. "We have water, Joe Tea, Pellegrino, Fanta, a random can of grape soda—"

"Water would be good. Thanks." I've been nervous all night about seeing Jude. I thought by now he would have told me why he asked me over. But he's acting like the last time we saw each other didn't even happen. Like he didn't walk out on me. Like we've been friends all along. Or . . . whatever we are.

"Or I can make coffee?" Jude offers.

"I'm good with water."

"Okay, but I need a caffeine hit." Jude selects a K-Cup for the Keurig. He is probably going for Italian dark roast if he has any. I love that I know those kinds of details about him. I know he got that scar above his left eye from falling off his bike when he was nine. I know his first crush was Samantha Rutherford in fourth grade. I know he first saw Blue Man Group when his mom took him, which inspired his passion for performance art. I love all these little things that make Jude who he is. And I want to find out much more. I want to know everything there is to know about this boy.

We take our water and coffee back to the cozy couch corner. We're in the middle of a conversation about how David Blaine held his breath for seventeen minutes and four seconds when I dare to speak the unspoken question.

"Can I ask you something?" I say.

"Shoot."

My mouth is dry. I take another sip of water. "Why did you ask me to come here?"

"To my office?"

"Yeah."

"Why not?"

"No, I mean . . . why did you even call me? It sounded like you didn't want me in your life anymore the last time I saw you. What changed?"

"I don't know. I was sitting here at my desk last night, remembering how I was telling you about my meeting with potential investors on our second date. I didn't know whether my idea would take off or they would laugh in my face or what. And now look. Everything changed so fast." Jude blows on his coffee. "You were excited for me, and your excitement made me work harder. You're part of the reason I scored those investors. You were in the room with me when I presented to them. Not physically. But your spirit was there. So I guess I just wanted to show you how it all turned out. And to say thank-you."

There he goes again. Enchanting me with his magic spell. But this is one magic spell I want to be enchanted by. Unlike Logan, Jude is for real.

"I would rather have you in my life as a friend than not at all," Jude says.

"Same here. I missed you."

"Not half as much as I missed you."

Wait. Did I agree to be just friends with Jude? And is that all he wants us to be?

Jude doesn't know that Logan and I aren't together anymore. Would he want me back if he knew? And if he did want me back, would that be the best thing for him?

I have to be careful. There is no way I am breaking this boy's heart again. Jude doesn't deserve for me to be reckless with his feelings. Telling him about Logan before I figure out exactly what I want with Jude would be selfish.

So I don't say anything. I just sit with him in the cozy couch corner of his new office, celebrating everything he is and everything he will become.

CHAPTER 15
ROSANNA

I AM TOO EXHAUSTED TO meet up with Sadie and Darcy at the Skyscraper Museum. After not sleeping at all last night because of the mouse, I just wanted to come home from camp and take a nap. But of course I want to see D more than I want to sleep. Plus it's Friday night. Friday night is when people go out to start celebrating the weekend. I do not want to be Lame Napping Girl. I want to be Fun Friday-Night Girl.

D's friend Jesse gave him a last-minute extra ticket to Imagine Dragons. I'm just meeting up with D at a café before the show.

As soon as I see him, I know something's wrong. D isn't waiting for me in the casual, confident way he usually is. He's all tense, sitting straight up instead of leaning back in his chair, his leg jiggling up and down.

He's not even smiling. D always smiles when he sees me.

"What's wrong?" I ask as I sit down across from him.

"How can you tell something's wrong?"

"Because I know you."

D stops jiggling his leg. He looks at me, then looks at the table. "I have to tell you something."

"Good or bad?"

"Not good."

"Oh." His tone makes my stomach twist.

"It has to do with Shayla."

A surge of adrenaline makes my heart pound.

"She . . . you were right," D says. "She wants me back. We were talking last night and she told me."

"What did she say?"

"That she's been nervous about telling me, but she wanted me to know she still has feelings for me."

D looks at me with wide, scared eyes.

"She thought we were breaking up," he continues. Is he defending her? "That's why she told me."

I am baffled. "Why would she think we were breaking up?"

"Addison told her you were going to break up with me."

"What?" I can't even believe what I'm hearing.

"I know. I told Shayla that Addison is a nutjob. But Shayla believed her. So . . ."

Ever since Addison confronted me at camp, I haven't heard from her. Her eerie silence has been creeping me out. I've been wondering what her next move would be. When Addison confronted me, she told me that she just happened to be at some club where Shayla was and that she told Shayla I was going to break up with D. But nothing has happened since then, so I thought she was making it all up to scare me. I can't believe she actually did it.

"What did you say?" I ask, dreading his answer.

"I told her Addison was lying." D's eyes aren't scared anymore. "Addison *was* lying, right?"

"Of course! No, what did you say to Shayla about wanting to get back together?"

"I said I was with you."

"And?"

"And what? You and I are together. End of story." D reaches across the table, holding my hand in his. "Don't worry about Addison. She's a freak. All that matters is that we're together."

D is making me feel a little better. But Addison isn't the one I'm worried about.

All the fun Friday night potential has been sucked out of the air. Emotional exhaustion hits me like a ton of bricks on top of my physical exhaustion from staying up all night. The Donovan fuel tank I was running on is empty. I need to take a nap. When he leaves for the show, I drag myself home.

It is hard to fall asleep. I can't stop thinking about Shayla. And even with the holes plugged up and traps put down,

I still feel like I keep hearing a mouse skittering around. I bolt awake a bunch of times until I give up and call my mom. I stay on my bed to talk to her just in case anything is running around on the floor.

Mom is worried about the mouse.

"Are you sure your super plugged all the holes?" she asks. Her agitation trickles through the phone along with the sounds of my little sister, Grace, washing dishes. I picture them in the kitchen on a typical night after dinner, Grace at the sink and Mom putting the leftovers away. My heart aches to be with them right now.

"I think so," I say. "We were up all night searching every room."

"You girls need to stay on top of this. Mice can be a serious issue."

"We will." I want to reassure Mom as much as I want to reassure myself. Even if I don't know how much our super cares about the mice. He seemed nonchalant, like this is New York City so what are you going to do?

Mom wants to know about camp. I'm thankful for everything she wants to talk about that isn't D related. When she asked how he was at the start of our call, I just said he was good and working hard. She likes that about him. I tell her about the potato-print banner we made in arts and crafts today. I tell her we had fried chicken for lunch because it's Friday and there's always something delicious for lunch on Fridays. I tell her about the herbs my kids got to take home from nature with instructions their parents or guardians can use to cook with them this weekend. I do not tell her about Momo. What I'm going to do to help her is still unclear. She seemed okay this week, but I know that these kinds of problems always come up again. The only thing Mom knows about Momo is that she's one of my campers. I don't want her to worry.

"How are things there?" I ask.

"Hold on." The background noises dim as Mom moves into another room. I hear a door close. Then silence.

"Mom?" I say.

"I'm here. There's something I have to tell you."

"What?"

"Aunt Irene and Uncle Ernie are getting divorced."

"What?" There's no way I heard her right.

"It was a shock to me, too. To everyone."

"Why? What happened?"

"They're not talking about it. Other than to say they grew apart."

"But they had such a happy marriage." Aunt Irene and Uncle Ernie cannot be getting divorced. That is impossible. They have been my example of a successful relationship for as long as I can remember. My parents also have a good relationship, but they haven't been together from the start like Aunt Irene and Uncle Ernie have.

My mom is technically my stepmom. My biological mother left when I was one. I don't even remember her.

My dad has some pictures of her locked away in his big black chest from college, but I haven't looked at them in years. She was pretty. She had brown eyes and long, wavy light-brown hair like me. Even in those faded pictures of her, you get the sense that she was restless. That she wasn't quite all there. That only parts of her were visible while others were blurry, just like in the pictures.

"It certainly seemed that way," Mom says. "But relationships aren't always how they appear."

"How could they grow apart? They're already adults."

"You don't stop growing just because you're grown up. People can find themselves when they're in their forties, fifties . . . even older."

"But I know they were happy together. It wasn't . . ." I am shaken to my core. I can't even believe we're talking about this. Because if we're talking about it, that means it's happening, and that is impossible.

If Aunt Irene and Uncle Ernie could break up, what does that say about any other marriage?

I remember that movie night when Darcy and Sadie and I were talking about affairs. I used my aunt and uncle as an example of a happy marriage. They were my role-model marriage. Now I'm doubting everything I thought I knew about the strength of their relationship.

Reading in bed before I go to sleep, I can't concentrate on the words. My thoughts keep drifting away from the story to the concept of appearances. How could a relationship that looked so secure be so tenuous? Is any relationship truly what it appears to be? I think about the other relationships I know. Sadie and Austin seemed incredibly happy together before she found out he was married. But they were happy. Their relationship was as happy as it looked. It's just that, from the outside, no one would ever guess how complicated things were. Darcy and Jude seemed perfect together, and I still think they were. But Darcy didn't want a committed relationship like Jude did. Their relationship still has potential if Darcy is willing to fully invest in it.

Then I think about D. How do we look to other people? I could sort of pull off looking like I belonged with him when I was wearing those clothes Darcy gave me. Now I can't even imagine what people think. Probably something along the lines of *What is a boy like him doing with a girl like her?* Or do people see us as a happy couple? I wish there were a way to find out exactly how we appear to the rest of the world.

Romantic relationships aren't the only ones that can have deceptive appearances. Take my relationships with my younger brother and sister. They are technically my half siblings, but they have never felt less than whole to me. Just like my mom has always been my real mom. Someone looking at our big family on one of those rare occasions we went out to eat would never guess the truth about us. When the seven of us were all together, we could cause quite a stir . . . in a good way. Anyone looking at us would see a happy family sitting at three square tables hastily shoved together at the pizza place, laughing over slices and garlic knots. Or confiscating the big corner booth at the diner, singing along with the jukebox. Or reading one another fortunes from fortune cookies at the Chinese restaurant, with a running commentary about how true each fortune is for the person who got it. No one would ever guess that another mother existed before mine.

What if they knew? Would that make my family appear any less happy? Would we seem suddenly tragic? Would our family be classified as a broken home? I think about all the Christmases and Thanksgivings and Easters we've had together. Mom always opens our doors to anyone without a place to go for the holidays. A few years ago, we had over twenty people at our house for Thanksgiving. Dad dragged the old folding table up from the basement. My brothers and sisters and I sat at the kids' table, peering at the grownups' table and dubbing dialogue over their conversations. We cracked ourselves up over the dorkiest things, like the time Grace laughed so hard at our little brother's impression of a spastic cat on the playground that cranberry juice came out of her nose. Or when my older brother and sister acted out that *Saturday Night Live* skit where Justin Timberlake was on a Bee Gees talk show. Or when the five of us did mash-ups of *Sesame Street* characters as commentators for the Olympics.

We've had our share of drama just like any other siblings. There are times my older sister and I will get in fights that last for days. Or smaller arguments where she'll accuse me of using her mascara or wearing her favorite fuzzy Aerie sweater. But underneath it all, we are a team. Our parents motivate us to be a force of goodness in the world. They inspire us to stamp out injustice whenever we cross paths with anyone being mistreated. We have always been taught to be crusaders of justice, gladiators for social change.

Underneath the surface, my family is as complete as it appears. There is nothing broken about us. I have been shattered in the past. But I am determined to put the pieces of myself back together.

We are all a collection of our past experiences. But who we were before doesn't have to define who we will become.

My stomach clenches when it suddenly remembers I am also supposed to be upset about the deceptive appearance of my own romantic relationship.

Shayla still loves D. And she's made sure he knows it.

I know D told me not to worry. I know he's my boyfriend, not hers. But the nervous fluttering tells a different story. The nonfiction underneath the fiction.

There was something more between them that whole time D told me they were just friends. I knew it. When D admitted that they went out in high school, I almost felt more validated than devastated. Finding out Shayla still has feelings for him wasn't a revelation. It was the truth underneath a lie I never really believed.

I want to stop being the paranoid girlfriend. Acting like a crazy person on a roof deck when Shayla calls or interrogating D after they hang out is not who I want to be. I want to be able to trust him. I should be able to trust him. If a girlfriend can't trust her boyfriend, the relationship is doomed. But now that my worst fears have been confirmed, am I wrong to worry?

I want to stop feeling this way. I just don't know how.

And I don't know where we go from here.

CHAPTER 16
SADIE

"YEAH, NO. YOU CAN'T LIVE here."

"Why not?"

"Um, because it's disgusting?"

Austin looks around the deteriorating apartment. "It's not that bad."

I gawk at him incredulously. There are no words for how bad this apartment is.

When Austin asked me to look for an apartment with him, I assumed he wouldn't be putting grungy bachelor pads on the list. I understand he has a budget. I understand rents in the West Village are outrageous. But there has to be a better place than this within his price range. There is no way I can let him live here.

"Did you see the bathtub in the kitchen?" I ask.

"Those old claw-foot tubs are vintage. They don't make them like that anymore."

"They don't make them like that anymore for a reason." Austin smirks at me. "I think it's charming."

"And I think you should take showers in the bathroom." I stalk over to the bathtub sitting right out on the kitchen floor between the stove and the refrigerator. The other side of the refrigerator is almost touching a couch in the tiny space Austin's broker, Maxine, keeps insisting is a living room. You can watch TV and get a cold drink from the refrigerator without having to get up. Sorry, but it doesn't qualify as a living room if you can reach into the kitchen from the couch. "How do you even take a shower in this? There's no rod or . . . where's the shower curtain?"

Maxine, a rumpled girl who doesn't look much older than us, speaks up. "You don't take showers in the tub." She indicates a rickety accordion partition on the wall, yellowed with age. When she opens the partition, a narrow shower stall is revealed. The shower is so constricted you couldn't even turn around in it.

"Seriously?" I blurt. I know Maxine is just doing her job, but come on.

"Where's the bathroom?" Austin asks.

"This unit doesn't include a traditional bathroom," Maxine spins.

"But . . . it has a toilet, right?"

"Of course." Maxine points at a small set of three stairs leading up to a raised platform just inside the front door. A paisley sheet is tacked along the top edge, hiding whatever is back there. I thought it was a pantry when we came in.

Austin turns to me. "I'm starting to see your point."

"Are you going to look behind the curtain? I mean, nasty old sheet?"

He lifts the sheet aside. Perched in a cubbyhole is a toilet all by itself. A roll of toilet paper sits on the floor. A plunger is wedged behind the toilet.

"Yeah, so . . . I'm going to pass on this." Austin grins at Maxine. "You said there's another unit to look at? Not in this building?"

"Um." Maxine shuffles some papers in a sloppy file. "I had that right here. . . ."

"Oh my god." I made the mistake of opening the cabinet under the sink. Chunks of plaster have fallen off the wall around the pipes. Whoever lives here didn't even bother to sweep up the broken pieces of crumbled plaster. Or fill the gaping hole in the wall. An array of roach traps indicates that indoor wildlife is an imminent threat to whomever dares rent this apartment.

"Here it is." Maxine reads the address of the other apartment for us to see. My optimism gradually filters back in as we walk the three blocks to that building. Nothing could be worse than what we just saw.

"This next apartment is a good deal," Maxine tells us as

we walk down Carmine Street. "It's eight hundred square feet."

"That's huge," Austin says. "How can it be in my price range?"

"It's not a typical unit for the building."

"Why, is the toilet in the bedroom?" I quip.

Maxine chuckles a little. I can't tell if she's laughing to be nice or because she actually gets the joke. The way she was pushing that crazy kitchen bathtub place, I have to wonder where she lives.

We don't have to take one step into the next apartment for me to know that Austin can't live here, either.

This is a basement apartment. It's this weird structure carved out of the cement, kind of like a cave with walls they tried to get straight but gave up on. The apartment is right next to the laundry room, which is weird. But the main problem with this place and basement apartments overall is lack of natural light. The whole big space only has two tiny windows placed so high up on the walls you can't even reach them. Which means if Austin lived here, he would never have any fresh air. No fresh air is a deal breaker. The rooms are painted a dark gray. The little bit of light straining from the lamps is sucked in by the dark walls, making everything even more depressing than it already is. And hello, basement apartment? That's practically synonymous with indoor wildlife.

"A great value for the location," Maxine says. "This is

by far the largest apartment I've seen in this neighborhood at your price point."

"It's big, but kind of dark." Austin turns to me. "What do you think?"

My hard stare at him makes it clear that if Austin rents this place, I won't be visiting any time soon. Or ever.

Maxine scrounges up one last listing for us to look at. We take a quick cab ride over to Thompson and Bleecker. The apartment is a sixth-floor walk-up.

"You might want to consider looking at more sixth-floor walk-ups," Maxine advises Austin as we get out of the cab. "They're typically at least two hundred dollars less than rents for lower floors. No one loves climbing those stairs, but you look like you're in good shape . . . and stairs are cheaper than a gym!"

Either Maxine is a legendary spin doctor or she is desperate for commissions. This is probably her first job out of college. Maybe she lives with roommates way out on Staten Island. Or maybe none of her clients have found an apartment yet this month. She could be worried about paying rent on September 1. It could be killing her to have to push these horrible apartments in order to make a living. You never know what someone else's circumstances are. I tell myself to be less sarcastic around her about kitchen bathtubs.

Maxine finds the key to the front door of the building. The stuffy hallway smells like mothballs and coleslaw. I am drenched in sweat from running around in this gross heat wave. None of these apartments have their air conditioners on, and this steep climb upstairs is not helping. I force myself to stay positive. We are looking for an apartment for Austin, who cares enough about what I think to bring me along. Anyplace might be the needle in a haystack. Including this one.

The three of us are breathing hard by the time we climb up to the sixth floor. Something is off about the configuration of the apartment Maxine is opening. The wall outside the apartment is different from the rest of the hallway walls. It's all spackled over with a hasty paint job. The color looks like that burnt sienna crayon I never used when I was little because it was ugly. The door to the apartment is weird, too. There's a tall gap under the door. Indoor wildlife could run in and out under the door with no problem. Shaggy black fibers stuck to the bottom of the door are blowing around in a draft.

"I can't get this door open," Maxine grunts. She shoves the key in the lock again, pressing against the door. "New locks. The whole apartment is new."

"It is?" Austin says. "That's cool."

"The landlord built this additional unit on the roof." She takes the key out and sticks it back in, finessing the lock more delicately this time.

"Wait, so . . . this apartment was built separately on top of the building?"

"In a sense. Got it!" Maxine pushes open the door to reveal a brightly lit apartment with polished new floors. But the floors are pretty much the only new part. The kitchen looks like we walked into 1923. The cabinets are cracked, the stove is crooked and burned, and the refrigerator is from the same era as that claw-foot bathtub. Everything is a different color and style.

"Why does the kitchen look so old if it's a new apartment?" I ask.

"I believe the landlord used materials salvaged from other apartments in the building."

Translation: This kitchen is a hodgepodge of garbage the landlord threw out when other apartments were renovated.

Observation: This apartment is a rickety mess slapped together as an afterthought, a random Lego fort pressed onto an already completed building.

Verdict: There is no way I am letting Austin live here.

I get why Austin wants to just find an apartment in New Jersey and call it a day. Searching for the needle in a haystack is never easy. But despite today's horrific display of jankety apartments, I remain determined to help Austin find his needle.

"You'll find a good place you can afford," I tell Austin when we're decompressing at The Uncommons after our busted-apartment search. The Uncommons is a board gaming café I found while I was on Sadie Time, making the most of being single. For a while I didn't think I would get back together with Austin. I loved the hardcore board gaming group he brought me to, but of course I couldn't go back there and risk running into him. So I researched smaller, more laid-back board gaming groups. A few of them meet up here, right down the street from that weird Lego apartment.

Austin moves his Ticket to Ride piece. He leans his elbow on the table, propping his chin on his hand. "How can you be so sure?"

"I just know."

"You have the Knowing?"

As much as I want to say that I do, I don't. The Knowing is one thing that cannot be faked. "Not exactly. But I do know that anything is possible."

"It might be possible to make that place with the kitchen bathtub work," he says. "Bathrooms are overrated."

"Really?"

"No." Austin winks at me.

"Whew!" I lean back in my chair. "I thought you were serious."

"That's because you're gullible."

"I am not."

"You kind of are," Austin says with affection. "In an adorable way."

We pick up our caramel lattes at the same time, smizing at each other over the foam. I think about what Austin said.

"Am I really gullible?" I ask.

"Sometimes." He carefully puts his mug down next to our game board. "You want to believe that everyone is good. When people talk to you, you assume they're telling the truth."

"Doesn't everyone assume that?"

"Not cynical people. Not people who think the world is out to get them."

"What a horrible way to live."

"Exactly. You would never choose to live that way. Your positive attitude is one of the things I love about you the most."

Austin doesn't know about the darkness lurking under the light. He doesn't know about my nightmares or the hopeless thoughts I have when I'm triggered. He thinks I'm sparkly rainbows and unicorns all the time.

I wish I could be that girl. Not in an unrealistic way. Not in a naive way where I think nothing bad can ever happen and no one has an evil side to them. Only so I could chase the darkness away.

It's my turn. I study the game board, strategizing where to build my next train.

"Hey," Austin says.

I look up.

"Thank you for coming back to me. I just . . . I love you so much." He blinks back tears. "I'm sorry. For everything."

I reach out across the table to hold his hand. "It's okay. You don't have to keep apologizing."

Austin looks at me with so much longing to make things right between us, so much affection in his eyes that my heart aches. A slant of sunlight catches his sky-blue eyes, making them bright with silver sparkles. In this moment, we are connected by a bond that can never be broken.

Four guys at the table next to ours are playing a complex game involving a ridiculous number of game pieces. One of the guys steals a glance at Austin. He's probably wondering what anyone could be crying about at Board Gaming Nirvana. But this is the kind of safe space you can let your emotions show without worrying about other people's reactions. Old-school board gamers can empathize with emotional turbulence. Other than that one guy glancing over, everyone else is so engrossed in their games, they wouldn't notice if a piano crashed in from the ceiling.

It's actually not as crowded in here as it should be for a Saturday afternoon. That's the magic of August in New York City. I enjoy the annual perk of having Manhattan all to myself at the end of the summer. No lines. No reservations. Even most coffee shops have free seats. The Uncommons is a small room, but there are three free tables. I make a mental note to add this little thing, being able to walk in and sit down without reserving a table in advance, to my list of daily gratitude. I've been practicing daily gratitude like *Your Dream Life* says to do. It is supposed to inspire genuine happiness. I'm hoping this habit will help me shine light into the darkness.

Austin wins Ticket to Ride. I'm happy he won. I feel bad that he's struggling with so much regret. But his regret is another thing I'm adding to my daily gratitude list for today.

"Should we play another game?" I ask. I could sit here playing for seven hours with him. We both could.

"Sure."

"What was the one with the castles?"

"Asara."

"Yes! Let's play that next."

This is exactly what I want to do. I want to build a magical kingdom with sparkly rainbows and unicorns. A place glowing in sunlight, shiny and bright, where everyone lives happily ever after.

CHAPTER 17
DARCY

THE BEST THING A GIRL can do when her life is in shambles is find comfort in her friends. Which is why I'm stoked for movie night at our apartment. Going out in this disgusting heat does not appeal to me at all. The second heat wave of the summer has rolled in and we are rolling out the air-conditioning up in Apartment 4A. Not sure how we're going to pay the terrifying electricity bill after blasting every air conditioner we have. We can worry about that later.

Tonight I don't want to worry about anything. Tonight is all about my girls.

"Does it still feel hot in here to you?" Rosanna asks me.

I look up at her from where I am sprawled on the couch. "A little."

"How is that even possible?" she agonizes.

"The living room unit can't handle this kind of heat," Sadie says from the kitchen. She's digging around in the freezer for the coldest thing we can eat.

Rosanna drags a chair over to the utility closet. She stands on the chair to get a big fan down from the high top shelf. "This is what we did back home," she says, setting up the fan on an end table. She stacks some books in front of the fan. Then she empties four ice trays into a bowl, puts the bowl on the stack of books, and turns the fan on so it's pointed at us.

"Old-school air-conditioning!" Sadie yells. "Our neighbor used to do that."

"How old was she?" I ask.

"Ancient." Sadie hands out Italian ices and spoons. She gives a watermelon ice to Rosanna, an orange ice to me, and keeps a lemon one for herself. "She lived alone. We were always worried that she wouldn't be cool enough in the summer."

"I miss central air." Remembering the big house I grew up in with its refreshing pool and perfectly regulated temperature in every room is like recalling snippets of a dream I had a long time ago. Will I ever be able to create a life like that for myself? Is that even what I want? Or will I end up like Rosanna, working extremely hard and barely managing to support myself?

"So what are we watching?" Sadie asks. She scrolls on her laptop, searching for possible movies to stream.

We throw around some choices. Every movie one of us suggests is shot down. Either one of us has already seen it or has no interest in seeing it.

"What about . . .?" Sadie searches some more. "I just saw a trailer for something that came out last year that looked good. But I can't remember. . . . Let me see if I can find it."

A minute later, Sadie screams.

"Our video went viral!" she yells at me.

"What?" I spring off the couch and dash over to where Sadie is sitting in the puffy chair, sliding onto the wide arm. Rosanna leans over on Sadie's other side.

"Look how many views it has! And all these comments!"

She's right. The video I took of her ranting how there should not be a Java Stop in the heart of the West Village is showing a sharp spike in activity. Sadie posted it like a week ago. There were a few views at first. Some of Sadie's friends commented. But this is insane. The video has over a hundred thousand views and almost five hundred comments. Some big site must have just posted it. That's the power of public relations for you. With the right exposure, almost anything can go viral.

The comments are fantastic. People are saying Sadie should do more videos. One guy said he would pay her to go out with him. There's a comment string of people organizing Java Stop protests in their cities. An old lady who has lived in the Village forever left a long comment lamenting the homogenization of this unique neighborhood. It wouldn't surprise me if she was Sadie's old neighbor with the fan ice.

Sadie responds to some of the comments. Rosanna and I tell her stuff she should write. We come up for air an hour later. I flop back on the couch and Rosanna crashes on a beanbag.

"You guys," Sadie says, flushed with the thrill of social attention. "Should I do a video series on New York life?"

"Yes!" Rosanna yells. "You can expose injustices people walk by every day."

"Java Stop." Sadie makes a checking-off motion in the air with her finger. "Check."

"Can I be your PR rep?" I ask.

"That depends. Are you expensive?"

"My fee is . . . one cold-pressed juice at Bubby's."

"Deal."

"Ooooh!" Rosanna claps, struck by a good idea. "Maybe Claire Danes would do an interview with you. We know she lives in the neighborhood. We know where she shops. We could figure out how to get in touch with her."

"Totally," I agree. "Stalking Claire Danes instantly made us BFFs." Rosanna is still basking in the afterglow of when we saw Claire Danes on the street and shamelessly followed her for a couple blocks. "But you were a fangirl before that, right?"

"I loved her in *My So-Called Life*," Rosanna says.

"Um, excuse me." Sadie puts her laptop aside. She perches on the edge of the chair, pinning Rosanna to the spot with blazing eyes. "*Obsessed* with *My So-Called Life*. I cannot even tell you how many times I've watched those eps."

"Remember the one with the substitute English teacher who throws their papers out the window?"

"I know! And the one where Angela thinks 'Red' is about her?"

Rosanna pauses. "I'm not sure if I saw that one."

"Wait. You haven't seen all the eps?"

"No. I've seen like . . . four or five."

Sadie gapes at Rosanna. "Did you see the one where Brian writes that note?"

"What note?"

Sadie turns her gape to me.

"Don't look at me," I say. "I have no idea what you people are talking about."

"Okay, no." Sadie goes to her room. We hear her rummaging for something in her closet, moving stuff around. She comes back to the living room, proudly hoisting a DVD box set over her head like a trophy. "This is entirely unacceptable and cannot continue. We are binge watching *My So-Called Life* for movie night. From the beginning."

Sadie fires up the pilot. I really hope I like this show. Sadie is being so bossy she might make me keep watching even if I hate it. I catch her sneaking peeks at me while we're watching, trying to gauge my expression to see if I like it. Fortunately for both of us, I do.

Mental note: Find a boy who leans like Jordan Catalano.

We watch the first three episodes before I even realize what happened. Damn this show is good. Why isn't anything like this on TV anymore? Television has devolved into too much reality nonsense that is anything but realistic. This show is so real I get goose bumps at the end of the third episode, which involves my favorite character, Rickie, and a gun at school. But the one where Jordan will only make out with Angela in the boiler room and ignores her everywhere else wins me over as the newest *MSCL* cult fangirl. Jordan eventually gets his act together enough to hold hands with Angela as they walk down the hall at school. I have to say, watching that scene even makes *me* believe boys can change.

"Oh my god," Sadie says as the credits roll. She presses pause instead of going on to the next episode. She looks at me, all swept away by the romance. "Don't you love this?"

"I do. It's amazing."

"How could I not have seen this one?" Rosanna is aghast.

"Jordan Catalano is so sweet," Sadie sighs.

"Is he?" I wonder.

"Hello! Holding Angela's hand was huge. It was a grand gesture for him."

"A grand gesture for Jordan Catalano would be basic behavior for any other boy," I argue. "Why are we grading him on some scale for slackers? Was holding Angela's hand a grand gesture or like the simplest thing he could have possibly done?"

"But we know he means it," Rosanna says. "Not like . . ." She shifts on the beanbag, hugging her knees to her chest.

"Not like what?" I prod.

"Forget it."

"No, what were you going to say?"

Rosanna glances at Sadie. "Well . . . when Logan showed up, we thought it was a grand gesture. So I think the intention behind the act is more important than the act." She presses her lips together, shooting me an apologetic look. "Sorry for bringing him up."

"It's fine." I sit up on the couch and reach over to the end table, readjusting the fan. It does seem a little cooler in here.

"At least with Jordan we know he wants to be with Angela," Rosanna continues. "He's just struggling with himself. It's not like he's struggling with feelings he has for another girl." She rips the elastic out of her ponytail, her long wavy hair falling around her shoulders in an exhausted heap. Then she gathers her hair up into a tighter ponytail. Sadie and I know Rosanna well enough by now that we recognize her signs of distress. Yanking hair down + scraping it back up = bothered.

She wrestles to tighten the elastic around her hair.

"What's wrong?" Sadie asks.

Rosanna secures the elastic around a higher ponytail. Her arms drop to her sides. "Everything," she breathes.

"Boys," I say. "Boys make everything way more complicated than it has to be."

"If D were like Jordan Catalano, I wouldn't be afraid he's with the wrong person."

"What do you mean?"

Rosanna gestures desperately at the paused screen. "Jordan isn't treating Angela how she deserves to be treated. But we still love him because he's making progress. He's conflicted, but it's okay because his conflict is only within himself." Rosanna hugs her knees to her chest again. "D is amazing to me. He treats me better than I deserve. He keeps saying he and Shayla are just friends. But they used to be a couple. And Shayla still has feelings for him." Rosanna fills us in on what D told her last night about Shayla wanting him back. I knew that girl could not be trusted. And Addison is just ridiculous. What the eff is her deal? "It just makes me wonder if he still has feelings for her, even though he denies it. Maybe he does and he's conflicted about having feelings for two girls. Maybe that's why he's treating me so well . . . like he's trying to force himself to fall in love with me and forget about her."

"No, because then he wouldn't be hanging out with her," Sadie says. "He would stay away from her and focus more on you."

"It just seems like he still has feelings for her."

"How can you tell?"

"He would do anything for her. The way he ran off to help her when we were on his sundeck? Or how he always gets together whenever she wants, even if it means not seeing me that night? There's this way he gets when he talks about her, like he's trying too hard to downplay their friendship. It's hard to explain."

Sadie nods. "It's more like this vibe he's giving off, right?"

"Exactly. He can't help how he feels. He deserves to be as happy as he can be. I just think he might be trying to do the right thing instead of what he truly wants. Like I'm a . . . charity case or something." Rosanna's voice breaks.

"You are definitely not a charity case," I say, remembering how she threw the clothes I gave her at me. How she packed those clothes away and hasn't worn them since. It makes me sad that she won't allow herself to enjoy them, but I have to give her credit for taking a stand.

Rosanna looks at us, her eyes wide with fear. "What if he wants to be with me, but I'm not the one he loves? What if he still loves her?"

I can't with this. D sucks for making Rosanna doubt his

feelings for her. "Then he's obviously deranged and you'd be better off without him. Any sane boy would know that you are a catch."

"Which he does," Sadie adds.

"Anyway, tonight is about us," I insist. "And Jordan Catalano. I'm dying to know what happens next after his 'grand gesture.'"

"It's not what you think," Sadie hints, starting the next ep.

"Is it ever?" I wonder.

CHAPTER 18
ROSANNA

D WANTED TO EXPLORE THE East Village tonight. He's been feeling bad all weekend, ever since breaking the Shayla news to me. And he knows I'm totally worrying even though he told me not to. So he decided that tonight would be all about making me feel better. We had *pommes frites* at Pommes Frites with five different dipping sauces. We watched some cute birds in a little park. We found a lotion in Fresh that smelled a lot like the lemony minty cucumber lotion I loved from our hotel in South Beach. We're just walking around, seeing where the night takes us.

I am actually starting to feel better when a guy yells, "Donovan Clark!"

We look over at some people standing around outside a bar. D recognizes the boy who called his name, so we go over to him. D is smiling all big as they pound fists.

"Good to see you, man," D says.

"What's it been? Like three years?"

D turns to me. "This is Eliezer. I know this guy from high school. I mean, we didn't go to the same school, but his parties were legendary. Everyone was at his parties."

"I aim to please," Eliezer says. You can tell he grew up here. He has that effortless hipster look most likely funded by rich parents. Destroyed black jeans, a vintage band T-shirt, studded belt, high-tops that look like they're not from here. I wouldn't be surprised if he's wearing a thousand dollars worth of gear, strategically put together to appear like he just threw on whatever before running out the door.

"So what's up?" D asks.

"Not much, *papi*. Just waiting on—"

"Heeeyyyyyy!" A girl comes running up to Eliezer. She flings herself against him and grabs him up in a hug before I realize I know that voice.

And that pin-straight blond hair.

And that perfect size-zero body.

When she turns around and sees us, my heart sinks. Of all the places she could be, why does she have to be right here, right now?

"Hey," D says.

Shayla stares at me. She must know I know what she did. But she doesn't apologize. She doesn't say anything to me at all.

Shayla recovers quickly, aiming her high-voltage smile at D. "Hey! What are you doing here?"

"We just ran into Eliezer."

"Shut the front door." Shayla gapes at Eliezer. "He doesn't know?"

"Know what?" D asks.

"We're meeting up with Lemarr and those guys. Do you have plans?"

"No, we're—"

"Then you have to come in!" Shayla grabs D's arm and pushes Eliezer toward the front door of the bar. Eliezer shows his ID to the bouncer. Then Shayla shows hers. They disappear inside as if it's a given we will follow them.

My head is spinning from staying up until three in the morning watching *My So-Called Life* and then waking up way earlier than I should have. And now this.

"Is it okay if we go?" D asks. "Only for a little while? I haven't seen Eliezer and those guys in forever. We'll only stay for a few minutes, I promise. You'll really like Eliezer. He's hysterical."

D obviously wants to go. The last thing I want to do is get in the way of his fun. And like he said, we won't stay long.

"Okay," I agree. I try to sound happy about it, but I'm not.

The bar is packed. D grabs my hand and leads me

through the tight groups of people. I say sorry to a girl I bump into. She doesn't even notice me.

We find Shayla and Eliezer, who have somehow managed to squeeze themselves up to the bar.

"What are you drinking?" Shayla yells at me over the music.

"Water."

"What?" Shayla scrunches her perfect features into a confused expression. Is it because she didn't hear me? Or because she can't believe anyone would order water at a bar?

"She's underage!" D yells to Shayla. He holds up my hand, a neon-orange underage band dangling on my wrist. "She doesn't have ID!"

"Oh!" Shayla laughs. She says something to D I can't hear, then orders drinks for the two of them. Is she laughing at me because I just graduated from high school and they're twenty-one? She probably thinks D is ridiculous for wasting time with someone who can't get into places he wants to go.

I hover awkwardly at the bar while D and Shayla wait for their drinks. Eliezer is already talking to two pretty girls sitting at the bar. They're smiling at him and laughing at something he just said. Shayla has D engrossed in a conversation I can't hear. D turns halfway toward me with my glass of water, handing it to me with a tight smile. Maybe he's starting to feel like he's wasting time with me, too. Everyone around me is laughing and smiling and having a blast. I feel alone in a sea of couples and groups who are entirely in their element. It's the same empty feeling I had at Bryant Park movie night when I was waiting for my boyfriend who was never going to show up.

This has got to be the most crowded bar in the East Village. And the loudest. Three girls next to me in identical outfits of skinny jeans, stilettos, and shiny crop tops are laughing so hard they're shrieking. I tug at the hem of my washed-out black tank, wishing it were clingier. I also wish my jeans fit better. They're so old no one even wears this cut anymore. I watch the shiny crop-top girls, wondering why they think this is a good time. Is this what most people consider fun? Screaming at each other in a crowd so packed you can't move without bumping into someone? There is nothing fun about this. Even if I wasn't here with my boyfriend and the girl he might still be in love with.

D and Shayla twirl from the bar with drinks in their hands. They are effervescent, thriving, radiant twenty-somethings. I am the immature teenager tagging along on a grown-up date.

"Where's Lemarr?" D asks Shayla.

"Late. You know how he is." Shayla presses her lips together in a smug little twist.

I sip my water.

"So!" Shayla bubbles at me. "D told me you're a camp counselor. Do you love it?"

"Yeah. We have a lot of fun. The other—"

"Kids are so cute," Shayla cuts me off, swatting D on the arm. "Remember Lemarr's little sister? Wasn't she a trip?"

"Like the time she almost flooded the bathroom at Eliezer's party?"

"Yes!" Shayla squeals. "I totally forgot about that! With the Ashleys having a dance-off on the antique table?" She simpers at me, lifting her glass to her lips. "You had to be there."

She did not just *you had to be there* me.

D's arm is touching Shayla's arm. Neither of them seem aware that they're touching. They have this fluid connection built on a shared history and past relationship that is extremely painful to be around. They are completely at ease with each other, like touching is the most natural thing in the world. What are they like when they get together? Are they always like this? With the inside jokes and the effortless rapport and the constant touching?

I get the feeling they are even worse when it's just the two of them.

"How badass is Eliezer?" Shayla says. "He picks up not one but two girls the second we walk in and then totally ignores us." Shayla squeezes Eliezer's arm. "Making new friends?" she singsongs.

Eliezer turns toward us to introduce the girls. But I'm not really listening. I'm noticing more details about Shayla that I was trying to block out before. Light glints off her hair. Her glittery eyeliner is on point. Her deep-red lip gloss is so resilient it is miraculously maintaining its mirror shine with every sip she takes from her drink. The cheap lip gloss I use is splotched all over my glass. I glare at the smudgy rim of my water glass as if it has betrayed me.

None of this is okay.

The next hour is one of the most agonizing hours of my life. Eliezer follows the girls into another room of the bar. Lemarr is still not here yet. D and Shayla kind of include me in what they're talking about, but the conversation is 90% them, 10% me. Anyone watching us would assume that they are the couple in our awkward threesome. This disgusting tension keeps building the longer Shayla ignores that she tried to steal my boyfriend. The same boyfriend she's showing off her strong connection with right in front of me. D seems oblivious to how this is making me feel. His attitude is that I'm his girlfriend, so what Shayla says or does doesn't matter. But what's her excuse?

I watch D and Shayla as their conversation flows freely from high school friends to the new Lilly Singh video to that time Shayla flirted with James Franco. To D's family.

"Did your mom return that vase?" Shayla asks D.

"She donated it." D explains to me that the vase was a birthday present from one of his mom's friends who apparently has no idea what his mom likes. "How can you be friends with someone and think they would want a vase with dancing frogs on it? That's the kind of gift you would give someone if you want them to hate you, not be your friend."

Shayla's laughter trills like a car alarm over the noisy scene. A pack of frat boys muscles up to the bar, pushing me closer to D. I actually feel like I'm intruding on his date with Shayla. He hasn't touched me once since we got here except to lift my wrist with the underage band. One of the frat boys gives Shayla an appreciative look. He says something to his buddies. They all turn to look at Shayla.

But Shayla is looking at D.

And D is looking at Shayla.

The electricity between them is so strong I can almost hear it crackle.

My throat gets tight. I gulp down the rest of my water, mentally commanding my eyes to stop filling with tears.

Even though it only lasts a few seconds, the way D is looking at Shayla confirms everything I've been afraid of. I don't think he realizes what he is doing. He doesn't know what his face looks like, but the truth is written all over it. I recognize his laser focus. I never thought he would look at anyone else that way. That he *could* look at anyone else that way.

I can't pretend I'm the one he loves anymore.

D has never told me he loves me. We've been together for almost two months. I don't know how long boys normally wait to tell their girlfriend that they love her. But I do know that if he were going to love me, he would feel it by now. D cares about me. He likes treating me to nice things. But neither of those is the same as being in love.

As much as I love him, I deserve to be loved back. I deserve to be with someone who only wants to be with me.

I pull D close.

"I have to go," I say into his ear.

"Why?"

"I'm not feeling well."

D gives me a look like he knows that's not why. "Are you sure?"

I nod. If I try to say anything else, I will burst into tears.

"Hey," D tells Shayla. "We're taking off."

"Aw! Stay until Lemarr gets here?"

"Sorry. We need to go."

Shayla makes a pouty face that I want to hate but only makes her look more adorable. I'm sure her pouty face has convinced lots of boys to change their minds about lots of things.

"Okay," Shayla relents. "It was really nice getting to know you better, Rosanna."

Like she even talked to me for three seconds.

Shayla glances down to the other end of the bar, seductively tucking her hair behind one ear. We follow her glance. An incredibly hot guy is smiling at her. This guy is so hot I have to remind myself I'm looking at him in real life instead of in a magazine.

"Have fun," I say.

"Will do," Shayla says, locking eyes with the hot guy again.

There is a moment before D says bye to Shayla, a moment while he's watching her lock eyes with the hot guy, when I see it. A flicker of disappointment on his face. It's only there for an instant. But it's like D flinches when he realizes Shayla is locking eyes with someone else. He might not even realize why he feels annoyed in this moment. But it is clear that he doesn't like what he sees.

Before I didn't know where to go from here. I didn't know how to stop worrying about D's true feelings for Shayla. I didn't know how to stop being the jealous girlfriend.

Now I know. My next step is clear.

We slam into a wall of humidity when we step outside. I am torn. Part of me wants to go home and forget this night ever happened. Part of me knows that I can't avoid saying what I need to say.

I wonder which part will win.

"You okay?" D asks.

"Not really."

"Too much bar scene? Sorry we were there so long."

"It's not that."

D hugs me. "Then what is it?"

We are not going to do this here. Not out in front of a bar so noisy the yelling and music and rowdiness is spilling out around us on the sidewalk.

"Can you walk me home?" I ask against his chest.

He releases me. "Why don't we grab a cab? It's so gross out."

"I know, but I want to walk."

"Whatever you want." D smiles at me, holding my hand as we find a quiet street to walk down.

Two blocks later, I'm still waiting for D to say something about Shayla. He has been quiet this whole time.

"I didn't know it was your mom's birthday," I say, breaking the silence.

"I almost forgot myself. It snuck up on me this year."

"I don't really know that much about her. Or your dad."

"Do you want to meet them?"

"I want you to want me to meet them. I want the idea to come from you. Not like I'm forcing you to introduce us."

He nods. "You should meet them."

A group that was doing shots at the bar comes scooting around the corner, whooping it up. One of the guys stumbles and almost falls off the curb. His friend yanks him up.

"Wasted!" a girl in an alarmingly short dress cackles at the drunk guy. Although I guess they're all drunk.

We stop to let them pass. I look up and notice a gorgeous townhouse. I learned about these from Sadie. She pointed out a few during one of our night walks, showing me how townhouses are traditionally narrow with pretty terraces. This townhouse has beautiful flowers in its window boxes.

I climb three steps up its stoop and sit down.

"I thought you wanted to go home?" D says.

"Sit with me."

He does.

And then I begin.

"You and Shayla—"

"We're just friends, Rosanna. Nothing's going on."

"Let me finish."

D leans back against the railing. He waits for me to continue.

"I know you guys are friends," I say. "But you and Shayla have this . . . chemistry."

"We just hang out. I swear."

"But it's more complicated than that. You have this emotional connection that's more serious than anything physical. Your shared history is so strong it's intimidating. I can't keep up with your inside jokes. I felt like an outsider the whole time we were with her, like you guys were the ones on a date and I was a third wheel. You flow so well together. You're so cute it hurts to watch. The bond you have with her . . . we're never going to have that."

D pauses. "You know how much I care about you."

Sure, D cares about me. But he loves her.

He rakes his hand through his hair. "I mean, yeah, I

care about Shayla, too, but it's different."

"Right. Because you guys are a better match."

D shakes his head. "That's not true."

"I think it is. Actually? I know it is. Not just because she wants you back. I see the way you look at her. Maybe you don't mean to look at her like that. Maybe you don't even realize your face is giving you away. But your feelings for her are obvious."

Music from down the street gets louder. A guy riding a bike toward us has a boom box propped in his bike basket blasting Michael Jackson. The basket is one of those old plastic woven ones with daisies. The clash of the little girl basket and grizzly man radio is fabulous.

We wait for him to ride past us. After the music fades, D stays quiet. Thinking about what I said.

I bend my legs up on the step, hugging my knees to my chest. "I can't be with someone who is conflicted about his feelings for another girl," I say quietly. There is no anger. Only truth. "I know you didn't mean to hurt me. I know that. But you can't help how you feel. Or how she feels. She never stopped loving you. And you never stopped loving her."

D doesn't try to deny this. I see him struggling to accept what I'm saying.

My boyfriend is in love with his ex-girlfriend and he doesn't even know it.

"I can't do this anymore," I say.

D takes my hand in his, imploring me with a look so soulful I almost give in. "But I want to be with you," he says.

"You know how you're always saying I deserve the best? So do you. You deserve to be as happy as you can possibly be. I don't think you're going to find that happiness with me. I just don't fit into your life the way she does." As much as I want what I just said not to be true, I know in my heart that it is. The kindest thing I can do for D, the best way I can repay him for everything he's done for me, is to set him free.

This comes back to the whole appearance thing. D is a good-on-paper guy. We are a good-on-paper couple. But reality is the only part of the picture that matters. I was so caught up in how perfect everything appeared with D: his perfect apartment, our perfect South Beach vacation, access to the perfect New York City rooftop pool. Perfection is an illusion. I would rather wrap myself in flawed happiness than an impeccable mirage.

Right after I met D, I remember wondering if I would get to attend a fancy dinner party with him. Why was that prospect even remotely appealing? I can't even remember now.

I really did lose myself.

"You know I'm right," I say. "Even if you don't want to admit it. You know what I'm saying is true."

D gently touches my cheek. I don't realize I'm crying

until he brushes away my tears. "I never meant to hurt you," he says.

"I know. I watched you with her. I saw you struggling to suppress how you really feel. Pretending that you don't want to be with her."

"I want to be with you."

"But you also want to be with her."

D's eyes implore mine.

"Right?" I say.

"I guess I never got over her completely," D admits. "She was the one who broke it off. There was always a part of me that hoped she would come back. But that was a long time ago, and then I met you and . . . I really care about you."

I'm crying harder. A lady walking her dog pauses at the bottom of the stairs to look up at us, making sure I'm all right. I'm that girl. The one alarming passersby. The one crying on the street. Breaking up with her boyfriend when neither one of them completely wants to, but they both know it's the right thing to do.

Now I know what it feels like to be both grateful and upset. Of course I'm upset that D and I are breaking up. But at the same time, I am grateful that I'm strong enough to let him go. The best version of myself is not a girl who would try holding on to a boy who belongs with someone else.

D's eyes are bright with tears. We are the good-on-paper

couple, slicing our picture in half right down the middle. Words can be much sharper than scissors.

"I don't want to let you go," D says, crying with me. Crying for what we had, for what we could have become.

I don't want to let him go, either.

But I am already gone.

CHAPTER 19
SADIE

MY KNITTING CIRCLE IS MEETING tonight. We usually don't meet on Mondays. But Mrs. Williamson had to cancel our last two sessions at her apartment and she really wants to see all of us. That's what she said in her group email. That she missed us while she was away.

I can't say the same for Marnix. From how he ignored me last night, it seems that he would rather not have to deal with a sister. Or any family at all. Last night was Mom's second attempt at Sunday family dinner since Marnix came home. It was a total disaster. I felt bad for Mom. She put so much effort into everything, making Marnix's favorite dinner of baked ravioli and arranging a gorgeous bouquet of flowers on the table with her best place settings. She wanted everything to be perfect. But Marnix moped the whole time. He barely said two words to us. He did apologize to me right before I left to say sorry he was so exhausted. But he didn't seem that sorry. Mom told me he's been hiding out in his room again like he did in high school. As long as Marnix attends his required therapy sessions three times a week, Mom thinks it's fine to let him heal on his own schedule. She wants to give him all the time he needs to come back to life.

I work my knitting needles faster. I'm almost done with this Christmas present I'm knitting for Marnix. After struggling to figure out something he would want, I decided on Gumby and Pokey stuffed animals. He loved Gumby and Pokey when we were little. Gumby is done and I'm finishing up Pokey. Hopefully he will think they're cute in a kitschy throwback kind of way.

"Coffee's on," Mrs. Williamson announces, coming into the living room carrying a big serving tray with a coffeepot, mugs, cream, sugar, spoons, napkins, and a plate of carefully arranged spritz cookies. The cookies are always the same assortment: flower-shaped ones with rainbow sprinkles, long ones dipped in chocolate on one end, and circles with raspberry filling at the center. Mrs. Williamson is proud that she's been getting these cookies from the same bakery for twenty years. I can see why her bakery has been there for that long. Their cookies are delicious.

Six of us are gathered on the couch and armchairs around Mrs. Williamson's lacquered maple coffee table. Mrs. Williamson puts the tray down on the table and lowers herself into the big recliner where she always sits, her housedress settling against the worn velvet cushion.

"Thanks, Dottie," the oldest knitting circle regular, Mrs. Varick, says. The rest of us chime in with thanks, plus oohs and aahs over the cookies. It doesn't matter that they are the same cookies Mrs. Williamson always serves. The ladies always fuss over them as if it were the first time.

I am the youngest member of our group. By far. Knitting came back a few years ago. All these twentysomething hipsters started buying yarn. Sometimes you can spot a girl knitting on the subway. There are some younger knitting circles that meet in Brooklyn, but I like my little group here. Mrs. Williamson likes that I'm here, too. She says I bring youthful energy to the group. The ladies like to ask me for advice about what their grandchildren might like them to make, in which patterns and colors. Or they'll ask what some slang they heard on TV means. Or who the cutest new actor is. The ladies said I could call them by their first names, but I insist on using *Mrs.* and *Ms.* It feels more respectful this way. These ladies are like a second family to me. One bonus about staying in New York for college is that I don't have to leave them or my Random Acts of Kindness group.

We sip our coffees and nibble our cookies while we knit. There is lots of complaining about the heat wave, how hard it is to get around, and how high electric bills have been. There is talk of the grandchildren. There is discussion of the upcoming holiday season, even though it's only August. Their conversation envelops me like a cozy blanket.

"So, Dottie," Mrs. Varick says. She's making an enormous quilt from scraps of other quilts that have been in her family for generations. Mrs. Varick is knitting new squares that will go between the old ones, linking everything together. "Tell us. How is Vaughn?"

Vaughn is Mrs. Williamson's son. He was really sick a few weeks ago. Vaughn has been fighting cancer. When he was sick, Mrs. Williamson told us he said it was a fight he was determined to win.

Mrs. Williamson presses her lips together. Her knitting needles stop clicking. She rests them on her lap with the doggie sweater she's making for her neighbor's dog.

We all stop knitting to look at her. Mrs. Varick tried asking about Vaughn when she got here, but Mrs. Williamson brushed off her question, muttering about putting the coffee on. All of us wanted to know how Vaughn was, but Mrs. Varick was the only one brave enough to ask again.

"He passed," Mrs. Williamson says.

It feels like I've been kicked in the stomach. The wind is knocked right out of me.

"It was a long time coming," she adds. She does not falter. She does not cry. She just tells us exactly what happened, almost like she is recounting the medical history of a stranger.

We are all stunned. I can tell by the devastated looks on everyone's faces that none of us knew. This is why Mrs. Williamson canceled the last two gatherings. This is what she was dealing with while the rest of us went about our normal lives like everything was fine.

Mrs. Varick goes over to Mrs. Williamson. She bends down and gives her a hug. That's when Mrs. Williamson starts crying. But only for a few seconds. She pulls herself together, wiping her face and patting Mrs. Varick's hand. "No more tears," she says. "I've cried an ocean already. Enough."

"What can we do to help?" I ask.

"This helps. Just you being here."

"We're here for you," Mrs. Varick says. "Whatever you need."

"Thanks, hon." Mrs. Williamson picks her knitting back up. "Maybe I could . . . remember him to you? For a little while?"

The ladies nod encouragingly. "Remembering" someone to other people is old-school for talking about that person. It's a way of allowing their spirit to live on.

My heart swells with a rush of empathy for Mrs. Williamson. I recognize her pain. I know what it feels like to lose a part of your family. But her loss is much more ferocious than mine. Her pain is vastly larger in scope.

I'm still in awe of Mrs. Williamson as I am falling asleep later that night. The way she was so strong in front of us. Her determination to get back to her routine, to her life, after dealing with such a shattering loss.

Her strength is with me when I wake up screaming from a nightmare.

It is with me when Rosanna and Darcy race into my room, asking if I'm okay.

And it is with me when I tell them about losing the sister I never had.

CHAPTER 20
DARCY

I AM SO FURIOUS ABOUT what happened to Sadie's mom and sister I can't even. What is wrong with people? Like you're seriously going to be stupid enough to break out fighting on the subway with tons of other people around? Including a pregnant woman standing right next to you? Seriously?

My heart broke when Sadie told me and Rosanna how that guy shoved her mom, who fell and lost the baby. Sadie said she didn't want us to feel bad for her. No pity allowed. But I can't help it. Sadie is like the sweetest person ever. It's not right.

I want to go on a rampage. I want to school every dumbass in New York, in the States, in the world. I was shaking when Sadie told us her story last night. I'm still shaking inside.

I try to keep my voice steady while I talk to my mom. She has enough to worry about. Every time I've called her since The End of the World as I Knew It, she has sounded so sad. My heart aches when she cries on the phone. I hate that I can't comfort her in person. She has done so much for me. I wish I could do more for her.

Tonight is her last night at home. She has to move out tomorrow. How crazy is that? My mom, who thought she would live in the big, beautiful home she built with my dad forever, has to move in with *her* mom. My grandma, who never expected to have her middle-aged daughter move back home with her. Grandma sold her house and downgraded to a two-bedroom condo after Grandpa died four years ago. The extra bedroom was supposed to be for guests. Not her grown and married daughter.

Life is crazy and random and makes no sense.

Those idiots who pushed Sadie's mom aren't the only ones making me furious. I used to like people. But now people I used to trust are turning out to be assholes. I am so furious at my dad that my head throbs when I think about what he did to us.

My mom is crying on the phone again.

"I can't believe this is it," she says. "How am I supposed to leave our home? There's so much history here . . . all the memories we made. I've been walking around every room, taking it all in. Remembering when you were little. You used to do fashion shows for me on the stairs. You loved gathering your stuffed animals in the breakfast nook for tea parties. Or in the living room to play school. Do you remember any of that?"

"Yeah." The outlines of my memories from when I was little are mostly colored in by Mom's stories and photos. I can't tell if I remember playing school with my stuffed animals on my own or if I remember because of what she has told me. Memories can be erratic like that.

"Now I have to leave it all behind," she sobs.

Hearing Mom this torn apart is tearing me to shreds.

I hate my father. I hate him for destroying her. For destroying our family. And then running off to be with a family he likes better.

No one should get to do that. No one should get to build a family and then throw them away whenever something better comes along.

Mom must be so humiliated that she has to move in with Grandma. I put myself in her shoes for a minute. On top of her husband breaking the law, having an affair, and leaving her for another woman, she has no money left to get a new place of her own. She wasn't even allowed to keep the money she made from her own work. Are her friends being supportive? Or are they still the superficial socialite club I remember, where prosperity is a given and appearance is everything?

After Mom hangs up to finish packing, my brain jumps from one catastrophic thought to another until I can't take it anymore. Even if I wanted to be in the Now, I can't stand being in my own skin.

Then I remember that I don't have to feel this way. There is an easy way out.

Alcohol tricked me for a while in high school. It lulled me into believing that escaping to an altered state would help me deal with everything when reality was just too much. I learned my lesson the hard way, drowning in self-destructive decomposition.

But I don't care what I learned back then. All I want to do is escape into that altered state again.

That boy I hooked up with in the Gap dressing room gave me his number. I put it in my phone under Random Boy. I can't remember if he ever told me his name. But I can remember how he made me feel. That rush of excitement from the day I saw him in Self-Help at the Strand makes my heart patter. I liked what I saw and made sure he knew it.

I want to feel that way again.

I don't want to think. I just call.

An hour later we are tangled together on a couch at Epstein Bar.

Two hours later we are making out in a corner between drinks.

Three hours later we are doing shots of a fiery drink so strong it makes my eyes water before I even touch my lips to the glass.

I still don't know his name.

Somewhere in the part of my brain where logic is supposed to be working, I know I should stop. I should rewind this night to when I got off the phone with my mom and not call Random Boy from the Gap. I should not revert to my self-destructive wild child tendencies that got me into trouble back home.

But this is happening.

"Want to get out of here?" he asks.

The chemistry between us is too intense. I am powerless all over again, exactly like I was the day we met.

I should stop.

I don't want to stop.

I can't stop.

We grab a cab to go to my place. So I can bring home this person I don't even know. And that's when, with the traffic noises and flashing lights and people walking around in all directions, the weight of my new life comes crashing down.

I break down crying before I can stop myself.

"Are you okay?" Random Boy asks.

A stranger asking me this in the back of a cab while I'm bawling makes me cry even harder.

The driver peers at us in the rearview mirror.

"She okay?" he asks.

"We'll get out here." Random Boy pays for the ride and we get out. He takes me over to a stoop between a psychic and a dry cleaner's, where I collapse in a wasted heap. He hugs me while I cry, sobs so forceful they are making my whole body tremble.

This is ridiculous. I don't cry. I mean, I try not to let unhappy emotions get to me in front of other people. I'm all for getting carried away with the happy feels, being swept up in the moment and letting spontaneous fun take me wherever it wants to go. But the rogue emotions, the ones that shove their way in after disappointment or heartbreak or anything else I don't want to face, those are the ones I try to push away. That is my version of damage control.

Now here I am crying over a new life I don't know how to live. And the old life that is gone forever.

"What's going on?" Random Boy wants to know.

As if I could tell him. I don't want to admit that I'm scared. I didn't even realize how scared I was until right now. It's like I've been running on autopilot ever since the day my credit card stopped working. No more money, check. Logan playing me, check. Get a job, check. Dad destroys our family, check. Mom has to move out, check. Jude just wants to be friends, check. I didn't stop to let anything sink in. Until now.

So I tell him anyway. All of it. Even the Jude stuff.

I never really got the help I needed back home. I thought I could help myself. This summer was supposed to be all about having fun and forgetting everything else. But what about now? I am wasted. I am disgusting. Falling back into old habits that lead to nowhere.

Random Boy is almost as wasted as I am. Or he was. Listening to the gory details of my miserable new reality has sobered him up. I can see in his eyes that I am not okay. He thought I was the uncomplicated girl, the no-strings girl he could have fun with and not worry about calling the next day. But now he knows I am someone else. I'm the girl who is just starting to see what a mess she is.

When we get up to leave and I fall down hard on the sidewalk, I realize this is what it feels like to hit bottom.

Everyone's bottom is different. Tasting the sidewalk is mine.

CHAPTER 21
ROSANNA

WAS SUNDAY NIGHT ONLY THREE days ago? It seems like breaking up with D happened forever ago. Or in another life. Or in a dream.

It doesn't feel real.

I've been crying on and off since the breakup. It feels like my insides were scooped out, leaving me hollow and shaky. The shaky sensation comes without warning. One minute I'll be fine, helping my campers put pinwheels together in arts and crafts or make milk carton micro-environments in nature, and the next thing I know my stomach will drop thirty stories like I'm falling off the ledge of a roof I forgot I was balanced on.

Breaking up with D was the right thing to do. I know that. And I know I will be okay. I just need to get my shaky legs on solid ground.

Momo isn't in the cafeteria having breakfast with Jenny this morning. She hasn't been at camp for the past two days. My stomach was in knots when I didn't see her on Monday. The knots tightened when she wasn't here on Tuesday. But I couldn't tell if my stomach knots were part of my breakup queasiness or something else.

Now I know it was something else. Something is wrong.

"Hey, Jenny." I sit on the bench across from her. Jenny's waffles smell really good. "Do you talk to Momo outside of camp?"

"No. Where is she? I want to show her the shirts we made in arts and crafts."

"I don't know where she is. Did she say anything to you last week about going away or something?"

Jenny shakes her head, sipping through the straw in her chocolate milk.

"Did she ever say anything to you about missing school last year?"

Jenny thinks. "She told me one time she got in trouble and missed a week of school."

"A whole week?"

"Yeah. It was her punishment."

"For what?"

"I don't know."

"Did she say who punished her?"

"She just said that sometimes she gets put away when he's angry."

"He who?"

Jenny shrugs. She pours more syrup on her waffles, making slow spiral patterns from the edges to the center.

"Jenny." I lean in over the table. "This is important. If you can tell me anything about Momo, anything that might help me figure out why she hasn't been here, you should tell me now."

She puts her fork down. She doesn't look at me.

"Anything," I beg.

"It's a secret," Jenny tells her waffles.

"That's okay. You can tell me anyway. Momo will understand."

"How do you know?"

"You know how you said she might be in trouble? Well, if she is, this is our chance to help her. But I need to know what she told you."

"You want me to tell you the secret."

"Yes."

"If she finds out I told you, will you say I was going to get in trouble if I didn't tell you?"

"Sure."

"And that I didn't have a choice?"

"Okay."

Jenny looks around. None of the other campers or counselors are close enough to hear.

She looks me in the eye. "The man who punishes her is her mom's boyfriend."

My heart thumps against my chest. "Does he live with them?"

"Sometimes he stays with Momo when her mom goes away."

"Is her mom away now?"

"I don't know."

"Does her mom know that he's punishing her?"

"I don't know." Jenny's eyes fill with tears. "Is she going to be okay?"

"Yes. I'm taking care of it." I come around the table and lean down to give Jenny a hug. "Thank you for telling me the secret. You did the right thing. Don't worry, okay?"

Jenny nods against my shoulder. But of course she's worried. So am I.

The bell rings for first period. I tell Jenny to let the other counselors know I had to go to the main office. Then I run there faster than I've ever run before.

Cecelia is on the phone at her desk. I fidget impatiently, willing whoever is on the other end of her call to wrap it up. When a camper is not going to be at camp, a parent or guardian has to call before camp starts that morning to report the absence. Same with when a camper will be arriving late or leaving early. Cecelia can tell me if Momo's mom has called her out from camp at all this week.

I barely give Cecelia a chance to say hi to me after she hangs up before I ask if Momo's mom has called her out from camp.

"No, she hasn't," Cecelia says with concern. "I've left messages for her, but she hasn't called me back."

"Do you have any idea why Momo isn't here?"

"I thought she might be sick."

"Then why wouldn't her mom call her out? Or return your calls?"

"Her mom could be away. I know she travels for work."

"Where does Momo stay when her mom's traveling?"

"Maybe at her grandmother's?"

The sickening knots in my stomach are tighter than ever. Not over some boy drama that was everything three days ago. They are about a girl who needs my help.

Sometimes she gets put away when he's angry. What does that mean? Put away where? Is that where she is right now?

I remember the night I was waiting in D's lobby for him to come home. The night he showed up with Shayla. I remember promising myself that I would help Momo no matter what it takes. When I think about victims who never see justice, especially kids who are abused, I become infuriated to the brink of insanity. I would do anything to help them.

Anything.

Including going back to Momo's apartment. This time I'll go during the day while her mom is at work. Or traveling or whatever. I don't know what I'll do if her boyfriend is home. But that's a risk I'm willing to take.

I tell Cecelia I'm sick and have to leave right away. She gives me a skeptical look, but says she will make arrangements to have other counselors cover for me. Like the last time I went to Momo's apartment, I don't want to tell Cecelia what I'm doing. I don't want Frank to find out I'm doing his job. He would definitely try to stop me.

Now that I have a cell phone, getting to Momo's apartment is a lot easier than it was the last time. I take the subway up to her stop and navigate my way to her building. This time the gritty neighborhood doesn't bother me. I am propelled across the South Bronx sidewalks by purpose and rage. Some guys loitering outside a dilapidated deli seem to sense my fury. They don't catcall as I blast by.

I recognize Momo's building complex. Fortunately I have her address in my contacts, because all these buildings look the same. I stand outside the front door of her building for a minute, figuring out the best strategy. It would have been good to figure that out on the subway ride up here. But I was so frazzled with worry that I could hardly think straight.

Okay. Momo's mom probably isn't home. Her boyfriend might be, but he doesn't know who I am. He doesn't know I was here before. If he opens the door I could say that we heard Momo was sick and I brought over a get-well card from her friends at camp. Once I get inside, I could pretend I forgot the card at camp and ask to see Momo.

Through the glass of the building's front door, I watch an old guy with a cane step off the elevator. He pushes the front door open a little. Acting like I'm supposed to be here, I pull the door open wider for him. He doesn't say thank-you. He just wobbles on down the path.

I take the elevator to Momo's floor. There's a sign on the wall showing which way to go for different apartment number ranges. I remember which way I went before and force myself to take deep breaths. Breathing is a challenge in this hot, stuffy hallway. The knots in my stomach are so tenacious they're reaching for my lungs. All my vital organs are at risk. But I refuse to let fear turn me back. I ring Momo's doorbell, gulping at the stale air.

No one answers.

I ring her bell again.

Still no answer.

Except I hear something. I can't be completely sure it's coming from inside her apartment and not the neighbor's. But I have a really bad feeling about this. I have to get inside.

There has to be another way.

I go back outside and look up at the tiny windows, willing the walls to crumble apart and reveal all the hidden horrors they conceal. I orient myself in the direction the elevator faced when it opened on Momo's floor. Then I mentally retrace my steps to her door, figuring out which way her apartment faces. I go around to that side of the building. Momo lives on the third floor. A fire escape goes all the way up the side of the building. Climbing it up to the third floor wouldn't be that hard.

I close my eyes, picturing the sign on the wall that showed which way to go for different apartment numbers. Apartment 301 was at the end of the hall to the left. The numbers went all the way up to Apartment 350. Momo lives in Apartment 332. Counting the number of windows along this side of the building, I can estimate which windows belong to her apartment.

No one else is outside except for two middle-school girls talking on a bench. They look at me when I pull down the fire escape ladder. But then they go right back to their conversation.

The ladder pulls down with a loud clatter. I glance around nervously. No one opens their window to see what the noise was. The girls on the bench don't even look over.

I wonder how sturdy this ladder is. All I have to do is climb up to the second-floor landing, then take the stairs to the third-floor landing. I put one sneaker on a low rung and reach up, wrapping my hands around a rusty high rung. The hot metal burns. Chipped paint scratches my hands as I climb up to the landing. Once I'm there, I edge around the stairs, trying to be quick but quiet since I am right outside someone's window. My heart pounds with fear that whoever lives in this apartment will call the police. I lightly climb the stairs to the third-floor landing, holding my breath. Then I slink over to one of the windows that should be Momo's.

My fire escape plan hinges on one of these windows being open. I'm guessing she lives in a two-bedroom apartment. Her apartment is not a corner unit, so in addition to each bedroom having a window, maybe the living room does, too. I will have to figure out the rooms by peeking in.

"Forgot your key, girl?" a guy's voice bellows over to me. I look around at the windows of the next building over. There's a middle-aged guy leaning out of an open window a few floors above me. His coarse laughter echoes off the concrete surfaces. He has a baseball cap on, but no shirt. He seems harmless.

I give him a thumbs-up.

He responds with more echoey laughter. Then he leans back in and shuts the window. I scan more windows to see if anyone else is looking. If they are, I can't see them. The hum of a thousand air conditioners grumbles like an agitated group of protesters. The air smells like dirty fried eggs mixed with a smoggy, industrial stench. Between the oppressive August heat and my nerves sparking like a malfunctioning electrical system, I have to keep wiping sweat from my face.

The first window has a cracked, crooked shade pulled down almost all the way. I peek into the room through the gap under the shade. This is a bedroom. There's not much inside—a big dresser, a small nightstand, and a bed. I can tell it's a grown-up's bedroom by the empty walls and boring colors. I creep to the next window, which does not have its shade pulled down. Clearly this is a kid's bedroom. The walls are covered with finger paintings, drawings in marker and crayon, and a jellyfish painted in watercolors. I recognize the jellyfish from our Marine Friends Day in arts and crafts. Momo loved her jellyfish so much. She was excited to go home and hang it on her wall.

There it is. Her jellyfish. In her room.

The window is halfway open with the screen down. I wedge my fingers into the slot at the bottom of the screen and pull up. The screen doesn't budge. I pull harder. The screen skids up with a screech. I freeze for a minute. No one comes into the room. It hits me that I'm hunkered on a fire escape outside an apartment I'm about to break into. Is it technically breaking in if the window was already open, people have seen me, and I have reason to believe that a girl is in danger? Even if it is, this is an emergency. There's no turning back now.

I drop my bag into her room. Then I duck through the window. I swing one leg over the window ledge, slowly lowering myself until my sneaker hits the hard, olive-green carpet in Momo's room. I lean against the window ledge and pull my other leg in. I don't hear anyone in the apartment, but it doesn't feel empty. Almost like I can sense a presence here. I look around her room and brush my hands on my shorts, wiping away the grit from the window. The room is small, almost too small to be a bedroom. There's a twin mattress on the floor with a flat pillow, a rumpled sheet, and a blanket shoved into a heap at the bottom. There are a few tattered stuffed animals on the floor next to her mattress. The filthy carpet looks like it's never been vacuumed. A basic pine dresser sits against the opposite wall with a Hello Kitty lamp. I recognize the beaded jewelry and tiara on the dresser from arts and crafts.

My heart hammers as I slip into her mom's bedroom, the living room, the kitchen, and the bathroom. No one is home. Yet there's still that sensation of another presence here.

There's a closet by the front door. I open it, checking behind boxes and winter coats and a bike. I check another closet in the hall. I check the closets in Momo's room and her mom's room. Everything looks normal.

Maybe Momo's mom is traveling for work and she took Momo with her. But then why wouldn't she call Momo out from camp? Or return the camp's calls? If Momo's mom is away and her boyfriend is supposed to be taking care of Momo, maybe Momo is at his apartment. Would the camp have his address? Or at least his name so I could try to find out where he lives? It's like Momo has just . . . disappeared.

I inspect all the rooms one more time before I leave. I don't want to be here too long in case someone comes home. I check under the couch in the living room and behind a huge recliner. And that's when I see it.

A little trapdoor peeking out from behind a stack of boxes in the corner.

The boxes are heavy. I push and pull on the stack, but it doesn't budge. I have to lift the boxes one at a time to move them. The first box is so heavy I am yanked down with the box as its weight pulls me to the floor. It lands with a dull thud. Once the other boxes are moved away, I can see that the trapdoor has a padlock on it.

My skin prickles with goose bumps.

I pull on the lock to make sure it's actually locked. It is.

"Momo?" I whisper. "Are you in there?"

I listen. Nothing.

"Momo?" I say louder. "It's Rosanna. Are you in there?"

I listen. Nothing.

But then:

A muffled voice. Like she's trying to talk but can't.

Oh my god oh my god *oh my god*.

Momo is in there.

Locked.

In.

There.

I scramble up and search around frantically for the key. I check the messy coffee table, the shelves, the side table between the couch and the recliner. The side table has a skinny drawer I didn't even see the first time I looked. I open it. A tiny key on a SpongeBob key chain is there. I snatch the key, run to the trapdoor, and open the padlock. The door pops open to reveal a crawl space.

And Momo.

She is hunched right inside the door, drenched in sweat. It must be a hundred degrees in there. Her mouth is covered with duct tape. She launches herself at me, crying and making muffled sounds through the tape.

I carefully pull the tape from her face.

"Water," she says, her voice cracked and hoarse.

"Okay, I'll get you— How long were you in there?"

"Sunday," she says.

Today is Wednesday.

Momo was trapped in that crawl space for three days.

She throws her arms around me, clinging to me like she will never let go. She is trembling so hard against me that I am vibrating.

"I'm so glad I found you," I say. Now we're both crying. I try to calm down so I don't scare her. I lift her up and take her to the kitchen. With my free hand, I find the cabinet with glasses and fill one with water from the sink. She is burning up. She is so hot and sweaty I can't believe she even survived. "Drink this." I help her hold the glass up to her mouth. She finishes the water in quick gulps.

I bring her to the bathroom.

"Leave the door open," she says, getting on the toilet.

"I will. I'm staying right here." I turn away to give her

privacy. When she's finished, I scoop her up and we go into her room. The window is still wide open. If anyone comes home, I will scream and take her out onto the fire escape. Momo clings to me as I take my phone out of my bag and call 911.

"Nine-one-one, what is your emergency?" the operator says.

"A girl has been trapped for three days. I just found her." I give the address and apartment number.

Once the operator confirms that help is on the way, I carry Momo back into the kitchen as I answer the rest of her questions. The refrigerator is practically empty. I find a box of sugar cookies in a cabinet and give one to Momo. She gobbles it down. I wish I could give her something healthy to eat, but there's nothing fresh in this kitchen. Only boxes of mac and cheese, SpaghettiOs, and other processed crap.

I take the box of cookies back into Momo's room. We sit on her mattress. She eats another cookie, still clinging to me. We stay like that until I hear the first sounds of sirens in the distance. The sirens get louder. They are coming for us.

I hug Momo as she chews the last of her cookie, digging in the box for more.

"You're safe now," I tell her. "You're safe."

CHAPTER 22
SADIE

"HOW MAY I HELP YOU, sir?" the guy behind the counter at Florence Meat Market asks the man in front of me. I'm happy the man in front of me is finally getting his turn. Standing in this line for five minutes has nearly pushed him over the edge. His impatient sighs and grumbling are old-man New Yorker code for *get this line moving already.*

"Do you have my turkey?" he demands.

"Which turkey is that?"

"Look, I ordered a turkey!"

"Okay. . . ."

"Seventeen-pound Butterball!"

"When did you place your order?"

"How should I know?"

I feel bad for the guy behind the counter. While he's

dealing with the escalating turkey situation, a woman behind the counter calls my number. I'm picking up an order for my mom. She's been coming to this butcher on Jones Street since before I was born. In addition to Sunday family dinner, my mom decided that we needed to have dinner together tonight. She doesn't like the way Marnix is reverting to his old tendencies, locking himself in his room and shutting everyone else out. She thinks tonight could be a catalyst for some big breakthrough for Marnix. Maybe there's a chance that if she forces him to sit down for enough family dinners, he will do whatever she wants in a desperate attempt to make her chill.

But three hours later, chaos ensues.

The absurd thing is that we look like the perfect family at the dinner table. Anyone looking up into our window on the second floor would notice the meticulously set table, the lit white candlesticks at the center, the platters and bowls of food Mom spent the past two days preparing. They would assume we were talking about what we did today or sharing funny things that happened or maybe even planning our next family vacation. They would never suspect the reason Marnix is here. Or why Mom is so desperate to make everything appear normal.

Mom has spent the past twenty minutes rambling about her friend's son. Apparently he's finally dealing with his drinking problem.

"He goes to meetings every day," Mom brags. "He is

so determined to recover. It's inspiring, don't you think?"
She looks at Marnix expectantly.

"What is your point?" he asks.

"Easy," Dad says. This might be the first word he's said
since we sat down. When Mom gets on one of her ram-
bles, Dad kind of blends into the background, letting her
do all the work.

"Do we really need to hear some manufactured anec-
dote about a loser we don't even know?" Marnix glares at
Mom. "Say what you really want to say."

Mom blots her lips with her linen napkin, carefully
smoothing it back over her lap. "I am. I wanted to tell you
this inspiring story about a boy who is actively in recovery.
He's made a choice to get better and he's honoring that
choice."

"And what? I don't want to get better?"

"Hiding out in your room all day isn't helping."

Marnix erupts in a noise somewhere between a bark
and a laugh. "Unreal. You force me to come back here
when I wanted to stay in Arizona. Then you—"

"That was a decision Dr. Peck made."

"Please. You love that I'm back so you can monitor me
up close. Like I'm some crazy person who needs to be
locked up."

Mom shakes her head. She's barely touched her dinner.
"You're not crazy."

"How would you know?"

"Because I know you."

"Do you? You forced me to come back, but you're afraid of why I'm here. You're afraid to talk about anything real."

Dad stares hard at Marnix, but keeps silent.

Mom looks at Dad. Dad doesn't break his stare.

"You came home because Dr. Peck thought it was too soon to return to the environment where you got into trouble," Mom insists.

"See? You won't even address the reality that I tried to kill myself. You use these weak phrases like 'where you got into trouble.' How about where I swallowed a pile of Vicodin I scored from this kid down the hall because I didn't want to be alive anymore?"

Mom's eyes swell with tears. I want to reach out to her, but I am paralyzed. I didn't know how Marnix tried to kill himself. Mom wouldn't tell me when I asked her. The image of my brother alone and hopeless in his dorm room, swallowing pills, is excruciating.

Marnix isn't done. "You still can't face reality. What did you do when I hid out in my room all those times? Nothing. You did nothing then, and there's nothing you can do now. You're useless."

"Enough!" Dad slams his hand down on the table, rattling the silverware and making the candle flames jump. "You do not talk to your mother that way."

"So the way you talk to her is better? You guys live in this insulated bubble. Tourists take pictures of this building all the time. They would smile at me when I left for school like they admired me for living on this fairy-tale corner in the West Village. What a joke. You guys have this fantasy lifestyle people would kill for, but there are plenty of other kids around here who are a lot like me. You don't have the first clue." Marnix glares at Mom. "You try so hard to make everything look perfect . . . and for what? Who are you trying to impress? Who are you trying to convince? Is it that if you make everything look perfect enough, your kids will actually be perfect?"

"I never expected you to be perfect," Mom says. She wipes tears off her cheek.

"But you never expected me to be flawed, either. Pretending everything is okay isn't going to make me better."

"You have to make a choice to get better. You're already making progress. Dr. Peck says—"

"This isn't about Dr. Peck. This is about you. You never even asked me why."

"Why what?"

"Why I tried to kill myself. Don't you want to know?"

"I . . . of course I do. If you want to talk about it. You need to heal on your own schedule."

"Part of the healing process involves talking about the problem."

"You went through a rough patch. That happens to all of us. But you're getting better now. Your . . . issue is in the past."

"How would you know?" Marnix shoves his chair back from the table. He gets up and leans against the back of his chair, his savage eyes seizing Mom like a riptide, dragging her farther from shore. "You don't know anything about me. Not the real me. Because you're afraid to find out who I really am. That's why you let me hide out in my room all those years, right? That's why you never asked what was wrong. You were afraid of why I was so angry."

"That's not true."

"You didn't want to hear the truth."

"So tell me now."

Marnix shakes his head, walking away from her. From all of us. "It's too late now, Mom." We hear his door slam. Music comes on. And just like that, I'm sixteen again. Afraid of my older brother.

"It was horrible," I tell Austin later that night in my room. I could lie on my bed with him like this for hours. Austin on his back; me halfway on top of him with my cheek pressed against his chest, my arm slung over his stomach, one leg bent over his. We fit together like we were made for each other. "You should have seen my mom's face. She was totally devastated."

"What did your dad say?" Austin asks.

"Nothing. He goes into these weird silences when Marnix gets upset now. They used to get into scary shouting matches before Marnix left for college. My dad was always yelling at him. But ever since he's come home, it's like my dad's afraid to damage him any more than he's already damaged. Like one wrong word will push him over the edge again."

"Sounds like Marnix wants them to stop avoiding the real issue. Whatever it is."

"That's exactly what he said at dinner." I prop myself up on my elbows, looking down at Austin in the warm glow of the lamplight. "Enough about me. Did you see those apartments today?"

"Horrible and horrible. They both had sleeping nooks where the bed was crammed into such a small space, the only way to get in and out of it was to crawl in from the bottom. Not happening."

"You'll find your place soon."

Austin slides his hand up my arm. I get all tingly like I always do when he touches me. "Our place."

"Hmm?"

"My place will be our place. I'm not only considering what I want. I'm thinking about what you want, too. I want you to feel comfortable coming over . . . and staying over." His intense look is clear. He wants me in his bed. All night.

An image of us tangled in his bed in his apartment with no roommates makes my face burn.

I wonder when it's going to happen. Our first time. Will it be a night Austin plans with a romantic dinner and walk along the river? Or will it happen without warning when we least expect it?

Austin smiles at me like he is perfectly at peace in this moment. Just by looking at me with so much affection, he makes me believe that being with me is the one thing he wants most in this world. I smile back at him. I don't need a mirror to tell me we have the same expression. We are the same in so many ways. We understand each other on a level no one else can. That's the thing about soul mates. Our connection transcends the world as we know it. There is another plane of human existence, and we reach that mysterious realm whenever we are together.

Forgiving him was the right thing to do. We can be together exactly how we want to be, for real. Nothing can stop us now.

CHAPTER 23
DARCY

THE BRIGHT SIDE OF HITTING rock bottom is that things can only get better.

That was the fleeting thought I had when I woke up with the worst hangover of my life Wednesday morning. It was so bad I had to call out sick from work for the first time. My boss was concerned. Ever since I started working at Java Stop, I've been the girl who requests doubles and eagerly switches shifts with anyone who asks. That's why I am now the happy owner of six tickets to a burlesque show at the Slipper Room. This guy I work with went away a couple weeks ago and I took all his shifts. He was so desperate for me to cover him that he offered the tickets upfront. He had no idea I would have taken the extra shifts anyway.

So tomorrow night isn't just Saturday night. Tomorrow

night is Slipper Room night. It's going to be me, Sadie, Austin, Rosanna . . . and hopefully Jude. When Jude called me on Wednesday to ask if I wanted to get together Friday night, I was just starting to feel better. His call was perfect timing, literally a wake-up call. The horror of sprawling on the sidewalk instead of working 5th Avenue like a runway crept up my spine like the most disturbing slasher movie scene of all time. I no longer have the desire to let my wild child flag fly. That flag needs to be rolled up and packed away permanently. Or burned. Not that I won't go out for a drink ever again. But I am done with the comfortably numb.

I am done with trying to escape my life.

These past three days have been all about soul searching. The search for Darcy Stewart's true heart's desires was intensive, requiring the brightest flashlights, long nights plodding through marshland, and mental exertion so strenuous there were times I wanted to call an end to the search rather than push myself even one step farther.

But I didn't stop. I kept going. I thought about how my life was destroyed. About all the things I hate. About all the things I miss. And then I let those things go. Not forever. I learned the hard way when I moved here with heavy baggage that you can't resolve an issue just by leaving it behind. But for now, I have let go of my anger. It's the only way I can move forward. It's the only way I can build a new life all on my own.

First stop: Cozy Couch Corner. While most New York offices are dead on an August Friday, Jude's office is humming with activity this evening. Jude asked me to wait for him at the Triple C while he wraps up a phone conference with possible new investors. Then he's taking me to dinner. You know, like two friends who get together for dinner sometimes. Because that's what we are now.

Friends.

I still have feelings for Jude that he doesn't have for me anymore, but I should be happy that he is back in my life at all. That's what I wanted. But the limitations on our new relationship are making me uncomfortable. Not even the Cozy Couch Corner can relax me. I'm all wound up.

"Want some?" Dax is leaning over the back of the couch, offering me a bowl of microwave popcorn.

"Thanks." I take a few pieces of popcorn that I am too agitated to eat.

Dax leans one hand against the top of the couch and launches himself over. He lands on the cushion next to me. "Nice dress," he remarks.

"Thanks." Normally I would buy a new dress to celebrate being asked to dinner by the boy I am secretly in love with. But that was before. My new life doesn't allow for extravagant purchases on a whim. In a way, my new circumstances are making me even more determined to rock this backless little black dress and strappy gold heels.

Dax crams a handful of popcorn into his mouth. Or tries to. Popcorn scatters everywhere. "So what are you guys doing tonight?" he wants to know.

"Just going to dinner."

"You sure about that?"

"I think so. Why?"

"The way Jude was talking, it sounded like he had big plans. He's been stoked all day."

"Really?"

"Oh yeah." Dax crunches another fistful of popcorn. "He couldn't stop talking about you after the last time you were here. Which was partially my fault. I might have asked if you were single." He gives me a goofy smile to show that he's harmless. "Can't blame a guy for trying, right?"

"What did Jude say when you asked him that?"

"He said you were seeing someone. But there was obviously more to the story. You guys used to be an item, right?"

Another vestige of my old life. "Something like that."

Dax's expression changes from playful to contemplative. "Seems like some people haven't gotten over it."

"What do you—"

"Hey, sorry that took so long," Jude says, coming around the couch. He's holding a drawstring bag and looking more delicious than ever. He scans the scattered pieces of popcorn on the floor, the couch, and Dax's tech geek tee featuring Tetris graphics. "I see you've been offered our finest snack cuisine."

Dax nods. "When you roll with D-Money, it's class all the way."

Jude looks at the popcorn on Dax's shirt. "I can see that." He winks at me. "Ready?"

"Not yet. I have something for you." I gesture to the shopping bag next to me on the couch.

"I have something for you, too." Jude holds up the drawstring bag he's carrying.

"Mine first. If you can handle the magnificent wrapping job."

"Yeah, well, I have to get back to work anyway." Dax gets up, popcorn from his shirt showering to the floor. "My boss can be a ball buster."

"But I hear he's lenient about cleaning." Jude bugs his eyes at the mess.

"Oh, sorry, man. Did you want me to—"

"You can clean it up later."

"Copy that. Good to see you again, Darcy." Dax darts a look at Jude, then at me, then back at Jude. Abruptly, he returns to his desk.

"He's a piece of work, but he's brilliant." Jude sits next to me, putting the drawstring bag on his other side. "So what's under the magnificent wrapping?"

I give him the bag. He pulls out the *Princess Bride* tee I bought for him in June. He holds it up and grins at Inigo

Montoya with the big HELLO in bold type across the top.

"I love it," he says.

"I knew you would."

Jude beams at the shirt. "Thanks for this. I'm really happy we're friends again. Not that we were just friends before, um— I mean, I'm happy you're back in my life."

There it is again. Friends.

"You smell like coffee," Jude says.

"That would be my new perfume. Called, um . . . Coffee." Smelling like coffee is my new normal. But I can't bring myself to admit to Jude that my life fell apart and I just came from work. Not when Jude is so freaking successful. Not when there's so much I want to improve.

Outside is gorgeous. There's a cooler freshness that is such a treat after all the heat and humidity we've been enduring. The air smells like basil and lemons. I don't hear any traffic noises. This part of the Financial District is all twisty streets and secluded enclaves. Jude and I are the only ones on this block. If we stood still in silence together, focusing on the Now and nothing else, it would feel like this night belongs to us.

We walk a few blocks. Orange evening sunlight is making Jude glow. His glow is making me dizzy.

Jude stops in front of a Citi Bike rack. "I thought we could ride around for a while and find a restaurant we like."

"Um . . . " I peer down at my strappy heels. The farthest

I could pedal in these would be like two blocks before my foot slips and I fall on the sidewalk again.

"No worries. I got you these." Jude pulls a pair of silver Vans out of the drawstring bag. "Size seven and a half, right?"

"How did you know I'd be wearing heels?"

"Because I know you."

Everything Jude says and does keeps reinforcing my feeling that he knows me better than any other boy ever has. Including Logan. Did Logan even know my shoe size?

I stare at Jude, hypnotized.

Jude seems worried that I hate his bike-riding idea. "All the bikes have a basket in the front," he says. "You can put your shoes in there."

"You thought of everything."

"Except for a backup plan if you didn't want to ride bikes."

"Dude. Of course I want to ride bikes."

Jude laughs. "Then we're all set."

Riding up along the East River makes me think of two things. I remember how invigorating it was to ride on the back of Logan's motorcycle that night he re-created our first three dates, how free I felt as the night flashed by us. And I remember when Rosanna told me about the bike ride she took with D in South Beach. She loved how romantic he was. He really did try hard to love Rosanna the way she deserved to be loved. He just couldn't fight his feelings for Shayla. You always come back to the person your heart truly desires.

Jude doesn't have to impress me with grand gestures like trips to South Beach. He doesn't have to pretend to be someone he's not. Or pretend he still loves me when he doesn't. Jude wants me in his life and I want him in mine. This way we both get what we want.

The more I think about it as we ride up and down the streets, the more I think just being friends is probably for the best. Relationships are messy. They come with unknown expiration dates. They crumble apart in the face of complicated feelings or ulterior motives or the weight of heavy baggage. What Jude and I have now is so much better. None of those typical problems can break us apart. We want to spend time together. Clean and simple.

One hour and two bike rack exchanges later, I've almost convinced myself I believe all that.

We get off our bikes at South Street Seaport, deliver them to the nearest bike rack, and walk around looking for a place to eat. I am pulled like a magnet to this restaurant called Barbalu. We read the menu in the display case outside, standing so close we're almost touching. Electricity thrums in the space between us. Jude smells the same as always, but even better today, like his pheromones are churning out extra attraction molecules. I hold my breath, willing myself to stay still, not to fling my arms around Jude's neck and kiss him.

Barbalu turns out to be an excellent choice. We're seated in a rustic-chic back room with a skylight and lots of cute plants. I look up through the skylight at people's apartment windows. Living above a restaurant you can see down into might be kind of cool.

Jude and I talk nonstop, just like we did when we first met. Same connection. Same chemistry. The only difference now is that he sees me as a friend while my feelings are complicated, a commotion of multifaceted pros and cons clanging together underneath every word I say.

"So guess who got in touch with me?" Jude says after we've had the freshest watermelon sorbet in the world. Rosanna would be dying over this.

"Who?"

"Samantha Rutherford."

"Who's— That girl you had a crush on in fourth grade?"

Jude nods with more enthusiasm than I can take. "She saw that profile of me in *The New Yorker*. See? I knew she was still pining for me."

"Throwback moment," I say. But inside I am panicking. Does Jude want to go out with her? Is he actually right about her pining? "What did she say?"

"She wanted to get together. She goes to Hunter." Jude shakes his head in wonder. "I can't believe she remembers me."

The panic roils into a storm of jealousy. Friends aren't supposed to get jealous over their friends' girl adventures.

I try to keep my face neutral as Jude tells me about their conversation. Seeing how excited he is about Samantha fuels the storm until it takes all the effort I can muster not to spring up from my chair and run out the door.

Things get even more complicated when the check comes.

At the beginning of the summer, I would have snatched up this check and insisted on paying. But now I can't even afford a salad at Chop't much less dinner at a nice restaurant. Jude did ask me to dinner, but this isn't a date. Friends usually split the check. Fresh panic stirs inside of me. Now I know how Rosanna feels when the check comes when the three of us are out.

The check sits in its black folder on the table between us. Jude is telling me a funny story about how one of his vendors got an order wrong, but with the check and my panic and his pheromones all swirling together, I can barely follow what he's saying.

Jude slides the check in front of him and drops his credit card on top.

"We should split it," I offer, reaching across the table.

"I got this," Jude says. He puts his hand over my hand on the table. He leaves it there longer than he has to.

We look at each other in the dim romantic lighting. Classical music plays in the background. Glasses clink together. The smell of warm rosemary bread fills the air as the waiter places a fresh basket on the table next to ours.

I focus on the Now, on this moment looking into Jude's eyes. Between what Dax said and Jude's lingering touch, I'm wondering if this is more than just two friends getting together. Despite trying to convince myself that less is okay, my heart knows what it wants.

Back outside, we decide to walk around before picking up new bikes and riding home. There's a bunch of people dancing together in a roped-in area of a plaza. They all have big headphones on with different colored lights on the earpieces. Everyone is dancing, but I don't hear any music.

"Whatever this is, we need to be a part of it," I declare.

"I think it's Quiet Clubbing."

"What's that?"

"Sort of like a Meetup group. They have three DJs spinning three different styles. Each DJ is a different color and you can switch your headphones between them. So you can be dancing with someone and either listening to the same song or different songs at the same time."

"Love."

"A friend of mine DJed for them."

"Have you done it before?"

"No, but I want to."

Sadie would call this an adorable non-coincidence.

We sign in to get headphones. Then we join the party. At first we're dancing to different colors. We can't stop cracking up at our clashing rhythms. But then we both turn to green and stay there. The DJ is playing a club remix of "Lost Stars." We move to the music like flowing water. I remember how Jude's eyes looked like a clear blue sea I wanted to dive into on our first date. That's exactly how I feel now. Like I want to dive in with him. Except this time, I don't want to get out.

I lock eyes with him, our motions in sync, the cool summer night breeze on our skin, Adam Levine's lyrics blasting into our headphones.

Are we all lost stars
trying to light up the dark?

Clarity blinds me in a kaleidoscope of bright colors I never noticed before but which have always been right there. All that garbage about how being friends is better than being intimate if you want it to last is a joke. What's the point of feeling with limitations when there is so much more to feel? This feeling, right here in this overwhelming moment, this is what I came here for. This is what I was chasing with all those boy adventures. I just wasn't ready to catch more than I knew how to hold on to.

But now I am.

I am in love with Jude.

And I don't want to be with anyone else.

CHAPTER 24
ROSANNA

I'M KIND OF NERVOUS ABOUT tonight. This is my first time seeing burlesque. When Darcy told me and Sadie that she had free tickets to the Slipper Room, we were excited for a fun night out. But then I realized I might be watching women take their clothes off. All the way. That might get kind of weird.

To me burlesque seems a bit demoralizing. Even though the women choose to participate, aren't they still being objectified? Sadie disagreed with me when Darcy gave us the tickets. She thinks burlesque is the ultimate example of girl power. Darcy thinks it's a badass way to take control, not only of a room but of your life. So now I'm worried that she might be interested in doing burlesque herself. She would make much more than any barista job could pay.

The five of us got here early so we could get good spots

close to the stage. As we're standing in a tight circle waiting for the show to start, I tell them about Momo. Sadie and Darcy have heard this before, but Jude and Austin are aghast as they absorb the details.

"Wait," Jude says. "Her mom had no idea her boyfriend was abusing her own daughter?"

"Apparently," I say.

"That's messed up."

"Sounds like she's hiding something," Austin says. "How could she not know? She must have suspected on some level."

"That's what I said," Darcy chimes in. "What kind of mother doesn't know her eight-year-old daughter is being trapped in a crawl space?"

"It happens," I tell her again, just like I did the day I found Momo. "The police said abusers can be tricky about covering up what they're doing. And they're good liars."

"But why didn't Momo tell her mom?" Jude asks.

"One time Momo spoke up. She was too afraid to be specific, but she told her mom that she didn't like being left alone with the boyfriend when her mom went away because he was mean. The boyfriend found out and took away her jewelry box as punishment. Then he threatened that if she ever said anything again, his 'methods of rehabilitation' would get even harsher and everything else Momo had would be taken away."

"Charming," Sadie mumbles.

"He totally brainwashed her." I take a sip of water to calm down, remembering how Momo broke down crying during her interview with the police at the hospital. "He convinced Momo that no matter what she told her mom, he would say Momo was lying. He would tell her mom that she was a bad girl who did horrible things, and her mom would believe him because he was the adult and Momo was just a little girl."

Darcy snorts. She looks like she wants to kill him.

"He said he'd have Momo taken away from her mom and put in foster care. Momo got scared when he told her what foster care would be like, living in a strange room with a bunch of other kids she doesn't know. Moving around from apartment to apartment over the years with foster parents who would do much worse things to her than him." I remember how powerful it was when the man who was molesting me said he would hurt my little sister if I told anyone what he was doing. Those threats are so terrifying you go into lockdown survival mode. "He kept telling her that his 'methods of rehabilitation' weren't even bad. That they would work if she let them and then she would be a good girl."

"What the hell?" Jude looks even angrier than Darcy. "Where is he now?"

"They can't find him. A neighbor tipped him off when he saw Momo and me leaving the apartment with the EMTs. He's been missing ever since."

Momo was afraid to talk to the police at first. After the ambulance brought us to the hospital, she was admitted right away and assigned a room with ducks waddling across the walls and a teddy bear sitting on a big armchair in the corner. Momo was in bed receiving IV fluids for severe dehydration when a nurse in panda scrubs pulled me aside to let me know the police wanted to ask her some questions. It was difficult enough for Momo to let the doctor examine her. Now the police were going to make her talk about what she went through? I talked to Momo first, just the two of us.

"Everything will be okay," I assured her. I pulled the big armchair up to the side of the bed so I could sit right next to her. "All you have to do is answer a few questions."

"How do you know?" Momo looked so small under the covers, but she was already looking better than when I found her a few hours before. The nurse had given her a sponge bath after the doctor examined her. She was no longer sweaty or trembling, but she was still shaken up. I could not imagine how she must have felt, locked up in that crawl space. No wonder she didn't want to hide in the closet when we were playing hide-and-seek at camp.

"The nurse told me the police won't stay that long," I said. "They want you to rest and get better."

"No, not that. How do you know everything will be okay?"

I wished more than anything that I could guarantee no

one would ever hurt her again. That no one would ever hurt any kid in the world again.

"The police are here to help you," I said. "That's why they came to the hospital. They want to keep you safe so this never happens again. But they need more information in order to protect you."

Momo was skeptical.

"Okay?"

She nodded. "Where's my mommy?"

"She's on her way." I tried to not let anger show on my face. When I spoke to Momo's mom while Momo was getting set up in her room, her mom said she couldn't leave right away. She sounded upset, but clearly not upset enough to come running to the hospital from wherever she was. Her excuse was that she was in the middle of a meeting. I would love to know what kind of work she travels for that doesn't allow her to leave when her daughter is in the hospital after her boyfriend locked her up like an animal. That is not right. And it's not right that Momo's mom went on to say she had been okay with her boyfriend disciplining Momo if he had to, although she apparently didn't know the extent of his abuse. Her parents smacked her around when she was little and she turned out fine.

Obviously our definitions of "fine" differ. By a lot.

Talking to Momo's mom made me wonder how innocent she really is. Momo was so worried when she got her shirt dirty that time we were repotting plants, and she didn't want Cecelia to call her mom. Did Momo's mom know more than she admitted? Or was she too immersed in her own world to notice?

"Please tell me Momo isn't going back home," Austin says.

"She's staying with her grandma until Child Protective Services investigates her mom."

"Good. That woman is definitely hiding something."

Darcy and I exchange a look. The irony of Austin accusing someone of hiding something is not lost on us. But I'm really happy that Sadie and Austin have found their way back to each other. They are so cute together. They keep touching and kissing like the happiest couple ever. Darcy keeps stealing glances at them. It must be weird for her to hang out with Jude like this, when they are supposed to be just friends.

"Okay, time for a subject change," I announce. "Sadie, what are you doing for your next video?" I am amazed at how her West Village rant went viral. It really does make me believe that anything is possible. Especially in New York.

Sadie's face lights up. "I found this little satirical graphic book called *NYC Basic Tips and Etiquette*. It is hysterical. All the annoying New York behavior is in there, like getting on the subway before people get off or texting at the movies. I was thinking of trying to catch some of those examples on video . . . or acting them out dos-and-don'ts style."

"Yes!" Darcy cheers. "That would be huge!"

"Could you put in people who stand too close to you in line?" Austin requests. "It's like, *Why are you touching me? How do you have no concept of personal space?*"

"Done." Sadie beams at Austin.

Austin kisses Sadie. They are still kissing when someone shoves her way up into our group, bumping into Austin.

He spins around to see who bumped into him. I look, too, and it registers that I know her.

"Shirley!" I yell. "I can't believe you're here!" I almost didn't recognize Shirley out of context from camp. Without her camp clothes and long feather earrings, surrounded by arts and crafts supplies, she almost looks like a different person.

Shirley turns to me. But she doesn't say hi. She turns right back to Austin.

"You seriously left me for *her?*" she seethes.

Oh. *Oh.* Shirley is Shirley. Austin's wife, Shirley. Sadie told me her name a while ago, but I didn't make the connection. Now it all makes sense. Finding Shirley crying in the arts and crafts hut that day at camp. The problems with her husband she didn't want to get into. That must have been the day after Shirley confronted Sadie outside our building. No wonder she was such a wreck.

"What are you doing here?" Austin asks her.

"It's on your calendar."

"How did you get into my calendar?"

"Your password is still the same." Shirley glares at Sadie. "We weren't done talking. You brushed me off at your place. I have a lot more to say to you."

"You have nothing to say to her," Austin interjects. "If you have something to say, you can say it to me."

"But this isn't about you. It's about your husband-stealing whore."

Darcy and Jude aren't even pretending to give them privacy. They are watching this surreal scene unfold like I am, perplexed and fascinated at the same time.

"You do know you're sleeping with my husband, right?" Shirley fires at Sadie.

"We're not sleeping together," Sadie says, her voice surprisingly level. "And he's not your husband anymore."

"I'm sorry, did I somehow sign the divorce papers without knowing? Because last time I checked, they weren't signed."

Sadie is startled. This is clearly news to her.

Other people standing around our group have stopped talking. They are staring at the drama playing out as if this were part of the show.

"Can we talk outside?" Austin asks Shirley.

"What, first I'm not good enough for you, and now I'm not good enough to be here?" Shirley wobbles on her high heels, grabbing onto Austin's arm so she doesn't fall over. "This is a public place."

"You're drunk."

"You think?"

Whatever Shirley came here to accomplish is not going to happen. The longer she stays, the worse things are going to get. I put my hand on her back. "Why don't we step out for a minute? It's too crowded in here."

Shirley lets me guide her out of the room, then down the stairs, then outside. She sits on the dirty curb surrounded by cigarette butts and a bunch of potato chips someone must have spilled. I sit next to her.

"I can't believe this is my life," she says. "Why is this happening to me?"

I shake my head, racking my brain for the right words that will make her feel better. "Sorry I didn't know you were . . . I should have made the connection."

"You have nothing to be sorry for. I'm the one who should be apologizing. I ruined your night."

"No, you didn't."

"Uuuhhh!" Shirley rubs her forehead. "I made a fool of myself going up to them like that." She starts crying. We are back to her crying on the ground and me being useless.

"I don't know what happened," she says through an onslaught of tears. "At first I wasn't going to do anything. The plan was to come by and watch them together for a few minutes, just to see what she has that I don't. I was going to leave without them even knowing I was here. But then I went crazy when I saw him with her. That was the first time I've seen them together. It's one thing to know your husband is having an affair, but then to see how he was with her . . . it's like I came undone." Shirley scuffs the sole of her shoe against a cigarette butt. "The way he was looking at her is what made me snap. I couldn't stand all that affection. And when he kissed her . . . He never looked at me or kissed me that way. Even before we got married." Shirley swipes at the tears on her cheeks. I wish I had a tissue to give her. "That's when I realized she's better for him."

A rush of empathy tugs at my chest. Shirley's heartbreak is the same as mine. The boy she loved was a better match for someone else.

We sit on the curb for a while, me rubbing her back, Shirley crying her heart out. My heart is breaking for hers.

I don't know how much time has passed when she stops crying. She tries to stand but can't find her balance. I help her up.

"Can you get home okay?" I ask.

"I'll take a cab."

"I'm really sorry about everything."

Shirley sniffles. "Don't be. Did Sadie tell you I cheated on Austin first?"

"She might have mentioned it." I was wondering why Shirley would do something like that when Sadie told me. Now I can ask. "Why did you?"

"Cheat? I guess on some level I knew we weren't right for each other. I just didn't want to believe it. Why I went looking for answers in all the wrong places is beyond me. I obviously have a lot to work on."

Shirley hails a cab and opens the back door. Then we hug goodbye.

"Let me know if you want to get together after camp ends," I say before she gets in. I doubt she'll take me up on the offer, but I feel like I have to put it out there.

"Thanks for sitting with me," she says. "Oh, and preventing me from making an even bigger fool of myself. I really appreciate it."

"Of course."

"You want to be a social worker, right?"

I remember that time at camp when she asked me about college. Even though I told her about my career goals, she changed the subject before I could ask her the same.

"Yeah," I say.

Shirley manages a small smile. "You're going to make a great one."

CHAPTER 25
SADIE

ONE THING I LOVE ABOUT New York City is all its secret places. Not only are there courtyards and pathways you might only find if you look hard enough, there are secret places hidden behind doors right out in the open. You never know what you are passing when you walk by them. Anything could be happening behind those walls.

Beauty & Essex is a perfect example. From the front of the store, it appears to be a small pawnshop. A bouncer guarding a back door inside is the only clue that there is more here than meets the eye. I've heard about Beauty & Essex, but this is my first time here. The massive space behind that pawnshop back door is actually a two-floor lounge and restaurant. This place is so fabulous there is a bar in the ladies' bathroom. Oh yeah. With a couch and everything. You could sit and have a glass of champagne in the bathroom if you wanted to. Although I'm not sure why you would want to drink in the bathroom when there are two bars here, just knowing you could is badass.

The Last Blast party with my friends from high school had to be here. According to Darcy, anyway. All the research she did before she moved from Santa Monica is really paying off. Now that she can't afford the kinds of places she researched anymore, she is determined to live vicariously through anyone who can. Starting with me.

Eight of us have a long table against the wall of the main room. Beauty & Essex has a killer atmosphere, all sultry colors and deco accents. A 50s Hollywood vibe is meshing with modern touches. This is the kind of place where women wore real fur coats and men smoked exotic cigars way back when both of those activities were socially acceptable.

A classy setting is always appropriate for distributing warm fuzzies.

I give everyone the warm fuzzies I made for them after we order. The plan was to wait until later, but I couldn't wait. My friends love them, and I love thinking about the warm fuzzies in their dorm rooms across the country.

We're all dressed up for this special occasion. But underneath the laughter and the happy energy buzzing at our table there's a bittersweet tinge. We are planning to get together again when everyone comes home for winter break. But I know how uncertain life can be. This might be the last time we are all together.

Most of my friends are excited to leave New York. Growing up here is completely different than moving here from somewhere else. Kids who grow up in New York City tend to be jaded by the time they're nine. They have this "been there, done that" attitude by middle school. Events that would be treats for any other kid, like eating out at nice restaurants or going to world-famous museums, are nothing special for most kids around here.

I am so thankful I didn't end up that way.

As my friends talk about what they're looking forward to at college, I remember my Java Stop rant. Most of my rage was sparked by the transformation of historic Bleecker Street, once a gathering place for social activists and home to mom-and-pop stores, into what is looking more like a suburban strip mall. And it's not just Bleecker Street. You can see the shift happening in lots of different neighborhoods. I thought it would be really sad if New York looked like any other American city ten years from now. But listening to my friends talk about the new cities that will become theirs when they leave for college, I'm starting to see things differently. My rage over the Java Stop monopoly sucking up helpless little stores like a big bad boogeyman will never die. But hearing how excited my friends are to explore other cities is reminding me that every city contains its own beauty. Big cities and small towns all across America are each special in their own way because of the people who live there. The people who have made those big cities and small towns what they are today. My friends are going to become some of those people. They are moving away to create new lives for themselves, to contribute to new places in profound ways. They will fall in love with those cities, and that city love will inspire those places to flourish. City love is about community, no matter where you call home.

Eventually everyone breaks out into smaller conversations as people at large tables do. I'm telling Brooke about the wife drama last night at the Slipper Room.

"I thought they were divorced," Brooke says.

"So did I. Or I assumed they were by now."

"How do you feel about that?"

"I don't know. Austin has made it really clear that he's ready to move on. But Shirley obviously isn't. I'm kind of worried that she might keep . . ."

"Stalking you guys?"

"Sort of. I mean, she hacked into his calendar to find out where we were. That must have been how she found out what time we were having dinner when she showed up at my place. Wait, does it still count as hacking when you already have the person's password?"

"Yes."

"How will I know where she's going to show up next? What if she gets crazy, like Addison with Rosanna?"

"Who's Addison?"

"I haven't told you about Addison? Nasty Girl?"

"Uh . . . I don't think so."

"Oh, you would remember." I fill Brooke in on how Addison turned Mica against Rosanna and how she lied to Shayla that Donovan and Rosanna were going to break up. Then how Addison showed up at Rosanna's camp to confront her. Rosanna has no idea what Addison will do next or where she will show up. I don't want to live like that, constantly afraid of what Shirley might do next.

Shirley might show up outside my door again. Addison might continue tormenting Rosanna. You never know what could happen with Darcy. All this uncertainty makes me even more grateful that Rosanna and Darcy are my roommates. It was a non-coincidence that we were placed in our apartment together. We were all running from dark secrets of our past toward a brighter future we desperately wanted to create. But you can't just run away from problems. You can't resolve your problems until you deal with them.

It was time to tell Rosanna and Darcy about my sister. Darcy felt close enough to us to reveal what happened with her dad. Rosanna shared her darkest fears about Donovan with us. Maybe by opening up to each other, showing the parts of us we keep hidden from the rest of the world, we can help each other heal. We can begin to create the life we have been running toward.

CHAPTER 26
DARCY

"YOU GIRLS FREAKING RULE FOR rescuing me from Java Stop hell," I say as we're walking downtown along the water in Hudson River Park. "All work and no play makes Darcy a dull girl."

"Dull is like the last thing you would ever be," Sadie says.

According to Sadie, tonight is one of those gorgeous New York nights that are so rare in August you are practically forced to go outside and enjoy the weather. Tonight feels like a summer night is supposed to feel: warm, breezy, and bursting with infinite potential.

Boys walking or running uptown pass us in a steady stream of hotness. Most of them turn to look at us. Maybe because Sadie thought it would be cute for us to match. We're all wearing camis, cutoffs, and flip-flops. Some of the boys keep watching us after they've walked by. A lot of them are cute. But tonight isn't about boys. Tonight is all about girl time.

One guy around thirty running past us helicopters his neck so hard he actually stumbles. He puts his hands out to break his fall. Then he runs away, smooth move embarrassment drifting after him.

We crack up so hard we have to stop walking. I am bent over laughing. Sadie has tears in her eyes she's laughing so hard. Rosanna snorts, then clasps her hands over her mouth, horrified.

So now we're the main attraction. Older people are probably miffed at the three rowdy teen girls disrupting their nightly walk. Moms pushing strollers might see us and miss this time in their lives when they were young and free. More boys turn to watch us, a few of them smiling. We laugh until we can't laugh any more.

We stroll past the basketball court. Sports aren't my thing, but sweaty guys running around after a ball can be fun to watch.

"How's Momo doing?" Sadie asks Rosanna.

"Okay," Rosanna says. "Her grandma is taking good care of her. She actually *wants* to take care of her. So that's an improvement."

"I can't with her mom's boyfriend," I say. "How do people get that screwed up? Are they like born defective?"

"He could have been abused as a kid," Rosanna says. "Some people who were abused continue the cycle. It's their justification for not getting the help they need."

Anger flares inside of me. "What he needs is fifty years behind bars. Prisoners are nasty to child abusers. See how he likes being tortured the way he tortured that poor girl."

"I—" Rosanna starts to say something, then stops. We wait for her to go on. "I know a little about what Momo has been going through. I know what it's like to be violated by someone you thought you could trust. It messes with your mind."

Sadie and I look at Rosanna. She's made other references to some dark secret from her past she's been hiding from us. But she's never told us what happened.

"What do you mean by that?" Sadie asks her.

Rosanna focuses on the walkway. We slow down a little, but we keep walking.

"I was molested," Rosanna says. "When I was eleven. The guy was our neighbor . . . my dad's friend. I would go over to his house sometimes to play games. One time he kissed me . . . and it started from there."

"Oh my god." Sadie puts her arm around Rosanna. "Are you okay now?"

"Not really. I thought I was at first. I wanted to move to New York and forget about what happened. But there are all these issues that came up with D . . . trust and jealousy and feeling like I wasn't good enough, like I didn't deserve to be with him. Being with him made me realize I need to get help. Running from my problems won't make them go away."

"I was just thinking about that last night," Sadie says. "How we were all running from problems when we met."

I put my arm around Rosanna, on top of Sadie's. "'The best way out is always through,'" I agree. Robert Frost dropped some serious knowledge.

"Is that a power of Now thing?" Rosanna asks. I can tell she wants to change the subject. The last thing Rosanna wants is us feeling sorry for her.

"Kind of. I mean everything we do now shapes our future, right? So it's all about taking action now to make our future better." If having my life turned upside down, yanked inside out, and spun sideways taught me anything, it's that living in the Now isn't only about going with the flow like I thought it was before. You can't avoid thinking about the future and assume everything will work itself out. I have to make smarter decisions now. I have the power to build a stronger future all on my own, a life that I can be proud of. I am the architect of my own destiny. We all are.

"That's why Addison has been harassing me," Rosanna says. "The man who molested me is her uncle. My problems followed me all the way to New York."

Sadie's mouth falls open.

Rosanna continues. "She thinks I lied about the whole

thing. Spreading lies about me was her way of getting revenge."

"Why would she think you lied?" Sadie asks.

"You know how it is with families. Sometimes you don't want to see what's right in front of you. You don't want to accept the harsh truth about people you love."

Sounds familiar.

Rosanna told us everything Addison has done to her, but we had no idea why that girl was such a lunatic.

"Unacceptable," I declare. "I will bring the psychological warfare I was planning to unleash on Logan all over her lying ass. Just say the word and consider it done."

Rosanna smiles. "Thanks, but I have to take care of this on my own."

"Are you sure you don't want help?" I am so ready to throw down with Nasty Girl.

Rosanna shakes her head. "I'm good."

I hope Addison lays off. Rosanna's struggle is complicated enough without that wack job skulking around the city, perpetually fired up and ready to pounce.

"Actually, I wanted to help *you*," Rosanna tells me.

"Did you find me a new job?" I am desperate to escape Java Stop hell and find a job I actually like. I believe I would thrive as an expert sales associate at one of my fave boutiques. I keep checking in on them, but so far there aren't any openings.

"No, but it's related. I want to help you sort out your

finances. You know, ways to save and loans you can apply for if you need them and stuff like that. When you have time."

"That would be awesome." Rosanna is the most frugal person I've ever met. She can totally whip me into shape.

"It's the least I can do." Rosanna clinks her fresh rue21 bangles together. I persuaded her to trade the black hair elastic that was permanently glued to her wrist for some fun bracelets. On sale, of course. She might have the most frugal shopping tips for everyday needs, but I know where to find the fashion deals.

"The Zen garden!" Sadie yells. She loves this area of the park with its bamboo paths and stepping stones. Tall grasses enfold us as we walk up the path. Rosanna stands on one of the simple wooden benches while I jump around on the flat rocks. Sadie is looking up at the city lights. That same sensation I had outside Jude's office comes rushing at me again. Tonight feels like it belongs to us. We are young and free with everything left to experience in front of us. The kind of life that can only be yours after high school.

Back on the main path along the river, I bust out singing "Empire State of Mind." It came on when Jude and I were Quiet Clubbing and I can't get it out of my head. Sadie joins in. We're singing at the top of our lungs with night birds chirping and people staring and One World Trade standing tall and proud ahead of us. Rosanna joins in when we get to the chorus.

These streets will make you feel brand new
Big lights will inspire you
Let's hear it for New York!

I love how bonded I feel to my girls. When all the badness went down with my dad, I felt more alone than I'd
ever felt in my life. But Sadie and Rosanna remind me that
I have them every day. They don't have to come out and
say it for me to know that they are here for me, just like I'm
here for them. It blows my mind that we've only known
each other for two months. I can't believe how close we've
become in such a short time.

Eventually the path bends to the right, extending out
across the water. Sadie stops in front of a big brass plaque
on the railing.

"Let's make a pact," she says. She puts her hand on the
plaque. "We can each promise one thing we will do starting right now to create our dream life."

Rosanna and I put our hands next to Sadie's.

"You go first," I tell Sadie.

"Well, I've been working on living in the light. I project this eternal optimist attitude, but I don't always feel
that way inside. I want to be the optimist I project to the
world for real. So I have to let go of my rage that's . . . Oh
my god."

"What?" Rosanna asks.

"I just realized that rage is always bubbling under

Marnix's surface, too. Look what it did to him."

"Whoa," I say.

Rosanna and I are quiet while Sadie takes a minute.

"Okay," Sadie says. "I need to save myself. No more rage. I promise to focus more on the positive instead of getting upset over the negative." She looks at me. "Your turn."

"I'm going to bust out of my comfort zone with Jude," I announce. "I'm going to let him get as close to me as he wants. If he ever wants to again. I'm going to let him take me to emotional places I've never been before. I am not going to worry about how things will end between us. I'm just going to enjoy what we have, and make smart choices so what we have will last."

"Wait," Sadie says. "Are you saying you want an exclusive relationship with Jude? Like, official girlfriend/boyfriend status?"

"That is what I'm saying, yes."

Sadie and Rosanna pop their eyes at each other. They are thrilled.

"Finally!" Sadie says.

"We love Jude," Rosanna adds.

"Your turn," I tell her. I can't stop smiling. It felt so good to put that out there and to have my girls be all enthusiastic. I am tingling with excitement.

"Um . . ." Rosanna gets her thoughts together. "I promise to take better care of myself by focusing more on my health and wellness. And to take advantage of being single like Sadie did on her boy break. And to resolve the Addison drama so I'm not always worrying about what she might do next." She looks at Sadie. "Can you say more than one thing?"

"Yes, and those are all amazing."

I am so proud of Rosanna right now. I love how she's embracing being on her own. Time will tell if I'm right about the inevitable disintegration of all romantic relationships. But I know for sure that certain friendships are strong enough to last a lifetime. Like ours.

CHAPTER 27
ROSANNA

"SEE YOU TOMORROW!" MICA CALLS out to me as she leaves camp for the day. Sometimes we walk to the subway together. But today I'm waiting with Momo out front for her grandma to pick her up.

I wave to Mica. She felt horrible when she found out why Addison spread all those lies about me. After Addison confronted me and revealed who she was, I kept asking Mica to get together so we could talk. She kept ignoring me, but eventually she agreed. We went for coffee and I told her everything. Mica said she had a feeling something was off with Addison, but she couldn't put her finger on it. She was scandalized when I told her that Addison even lied about living in Mica's building. I am so happy Mica and I are friends again. Finding someone you have so much in common with, someone who gets you without having to explain yourself, is a gift.

"My grandma got me a new jewelry box," Momo says as we wait at the pickup area in front of the school.

"You told me. That's awesome."

"It's pink and purple like the one I made you."

My heart swells with love for Momo. Her mom's boyfriend took away her jewelry box as one of his twisted punishments, but Momo still wanted to give the jewelry box she made in arts and crafts to me. That's how I know Momo is going to be okay. Somehow she is still the same sweet girl who cares about other people. Even without the help of time or counseling yet, she is a remarkable survivor.

"There's my girl." Momo's grandma comes over and gathers Momo up in a hug. I can't stop smiling when I see them together. It is obvious how much Momo's grandma loves her, and Momo loves her back just as much.

Momo's grandma asks about her day. Momo shows her the lanyard key chain she made. Watching them interact with such affection makes me think of my mom. I miss her so much. I'm going to call her tonight.

"Thanks, Rosanna," Momo's grandma says. "See you tomorrow."

"Have a good night," I say.

Momo throws her arms around my waist and squeezes tight. I bend down to hug her back. She hugged me like this yesterday, too. Yesterday was her first day back at camp since the day I found her. Momo's grandma said she didn't have to come back if she didn't want to, but Momo did not want to miss the last week of camp.

I watch Momo and her grandma walk toward the subway. They are holding hands and looking like a cute family with no concerns. No one passing them on the street would ever guess that Momo had just been a prisoner in her own home.

Just when I'm feeling the victory of good over evil, I see her across the street. Waiting against the chain-link fence like she was before.

Addison.

Except this time, I am ready for her.

She crosses the street and walks toward me. As I watch her approach, I make a decision to not be afraid. With every step she takes, I become more determined to stand up for myself, to say all the things I should have said before. Regret over not defending myself the last time she confronted me has been burning inside of me ever since. I have replayed that confrontation ten thousand times, hearing her harsh words strip me of my dignity over and over, until I've become so furious I almost wanted to track her down and unleash this pent-up anger.

Now is my chance.

Addison is finally standing right in front of me. Before she can say one word, I rip open all the rage and frustration and pain I have been holding in. Not just at what she has done to me. At what her uncle did to me seven years ago.

"You don't get to destroy my life," I start. "You don't get to hunt me down like an animal and shoot me with accusations that aren't even true. I won't let you intimidate me any more or turn my friends against me or allow you to come to the place I *work with kids* and harass me. You're done."

Addison is verbally slapped into silence.

"Your uncle molested me when I was eleven. That happened. He touched me whenever he wanted, wherever he wanted. I couldn't do anything about it."

People are walking by on the sidewalk. They come close enough to hear what I'm saying, but I don't care. I would broadcast the specifics to an entire crowd if it would make Addison believe me.

I am not embarrassed anymore.

I am not ashamed.

And it feels like freedom.

My voice is strong and steady as I continue. "He said if I told anyone, he would hurt my little sister. So I kept quiet to protect her. But no one could protect me. What he did to me will affect my relationships for the rest of my life. That's not okay. You accusing me of lying about what he did is not okay. You need to stop harassing me and my friends and move on."

Addison has been watching me calmly this whole time.

She hasn't tried to interrupt. She doesn't look angry or smug. She's not glaring at me like she is out for more revenge. She almost looks normal. I don't know why I didn't notice this difference in her right away. I guess I was feeling the rush of standing up for myself so strongly it obliterated everything else.

"I believe you," Addison says.

"What?"

"I know you're telling the truth. I came here to apologize."

"Um . . ."

"Another girl came forward. She said the same things you did. But this time there was more evidence. Her family pressed charges against my uncle. He was charged with enticement of a minor . . . and now he's in jail."

It doesn't surprise me that he abused another girl. But I can't believe Addison is admitting all this. "Is she okay?"

"As okay as she can be."

I can tell it's going to take me a while to fully absorb what Addison said. Her uncle is locked away where he can't hurt any more girls. He will be flagged as a sex offender for the rest of his life. I hate that it took violating another girl to bring him to justice, but I am relieved he can't hurt anyone else. Good. Over. Evil.

"I'm sorry I didn't believe you before." Addison looks like a totally different girl this time. She is shaken and vulnerable. She is no longer coming across as Nasty Girl.

Today she is just a regular girl traumatized by a family scandal. "To you he was a monster. But to me . . . he was always my uncle, you know?"

Now I'm the one who is speechless.

Addison looks over at the elementary school where we have camp. "Part of the reason I was so angry at you is that it didn't seem like you were lying. I couldn't deal with the possibility that what you were saying was true. That this nice man I'd known my whole life could . . . do those things. He was there for me when no one else was. He was like a father to me. I couldn't accept that he would ever take advantage of an innocent girl like that."

Her gaze drifts over to me, her eyes glazed with tears and sorrow. She's mourning the loss of the man she thought she knew, now that she was forced to accept the harsh truth about him. I can understand how complicated this must be for her. In a way, her uncle was two different people. He convinced her that the charade he projected in public was his true identity. He fooled a lot of other people, too.

Not anymore.

That other girl who pressed charges is my new role model. She was confident the way I wish I had been. But now I also want to be confident for her. For the strength and courage she has shown. For every girl who was abused like we were and is strong enough to overcome.

We can do this. We are not alone. And we will not be broken.

CHAPTER 28
SADIE

BOSIE TEA PARLOR ISN'T AS fancy as it sounds. It's actually not fancy at all. Bosie is this cute teahouse on Morton Street that pretty much has any kind of tea you could want. The ambience is mellow and the good vibes are abundant. As a tea enthusiast, I love coming here with friends for long conversations. Of course I've already brought Austin here. He likes it, but he's not as into tea as I am. Same with Marnix. Which is why I was surprised when Marnix asked me to meet up with him here.

When I found out he was coming home, I wanted to get to know the real Marnix, even if he scared me. Not how I knew him back in high school when he would slam his door and lock himself in his room for hours, or get into crazy yelling matches with our dad, or pound the wall next to me, not even noticing that I was standing right there. Marnix had anger issues, but I never expected that he would try to kill himself. Was he suicidal back then? Did he try to kill himself before? What if he had tried back in high school and we had no clue? I would never forgive myself for having been oblivious when he needed me the most.

I want Marnix to know that I am here for him, and I want to make sure he's okay. Or at least on the road to being okay. As I sit at a window table watching our neighborhood ebb and flow, I realize that we are connecting as brother and sister for the first time after both of us have moved away from home. I wonder what our relationship will be like after college. Or fifteen years from now when we're grownups. Thinking about being in our thirties, probably married and maybe even with kids, is weird and wonderful.

Marnix lopes in. People are always saying how much we look alike. We have the same shade of copper hair and the same brown eyes. I think he's attractive, but he doesn't stand out. Average height, average build. He sits down across from me all casual like we do this every day. But I can't help being nervous. We were never close growing up. We just never had much to say to each other. The only thing we really ever had in common was that we both couldn't wait to leave for college.

"Have I ever told you how much I appreciate air-conditioning?" he says. Marnix hates the hot, humid summers here. He used to refuse to walk more than two blocks at a time if it was over 90 degrees. Maybe that's why he picked this place to get together. Bosie is only a few blocks from home. "It is disgusting out. How did I ever survive summers here?"

"I like how empty it is in August. We have the whole neighborhood to ourselves."

"Yeah, if 'ourselves' include the hordes of tourists."

My instinct is to keep defending my city until he gives in. Even a little. But I don't press him. There is obviously a lot going on with Marnix. He enjoys complaining, but at least he's here and he *can* complain.

"What the—" Marnix is staring out the window. An old lady is dragging an animal carrier down the sidewalk, scuffing along at the slowest pace ever. She is wearing white orthopedic shoes, baggy stonewashed jeans, and a chunky gray cable-knit sweater. In August. The animal carrier doesn't have wheels. But she's dragging it along as if it does. We can see a cat hunched down inside. I can't believe her cat is tolerating this kooky mode of transportation.

"Only in New York," I say.

"Classic."

"Don't you miss it here?" Marnix doesn't appreciate the local weirdos. But one thing I love about New York is how it embraces weirdos of all kinds. This city is all about live and let live.

"Not really," Marnix says. "We're not all in love with New York like you are. You and New York are inseparable."

"That. Is so true." Maybe Marnix knows me better than I thought he did.

A waitress comes over to our table. I order an almond cookie rooibos tea. Marnix orders a regular coffee.

"So." Marnix leans back in his chair. He stretches his arms over his head. "How are those Sunday family dinners working for you?"

"Not as well as they are for you." The second the words leave my mouth, I want to cram them back in. I don't want to say the wrong thing to Marnix. Hopefully he knows I'm joking.

He looks at me evenly, not mad at all. "Yeah, I haven't exactly been the easiest person to get along with. Sorry about that."

"No, it's . . . I know you're dealing with a lot."

"There's some stuff I never told you. Stuff you should know."

"Like what?"

"Do you remember why you were on the subway that day with Mom? When she was pushed?"

Memories of the day Mom lost our little sister are always percolating, ready to froth to a rapid boil at the slightest provocation. So it's odd that I don't remember where we were going.

"No," I say.

"Well, I do. I was supposed to be on the subway with her. Not you."

"What do you mean?"

"Mom asked me to go see Carla with her. I told her I didn't want to go. I mean, I never wanted to go, but I was being a brat that day and refused. So she took you instead."

Carla was an older lady Mom worked with at the W Hotel. After Carla developed a bunch of health issues, she had to quit her job. She was homebound after a while. Mom used to visit her up in Harlem. Carla baked chocolate chip cookies for Marnix and me when we were little. Mom said that Carla always cheered up when she saw us. So every time Mom went to visit her, she would take one or both of us along, depending on whether Dad was home.

"You weren't supposed to be on the subway with Mom," Marnix says. "I was."

A pot of tea and a cup are placed in front of me. A mug of coffee is placed in front of Marnix. Cream and sugar are put on the table. In a fog, I thank the waitress as the reason Marnix is telling me this sharpens into focus.

"There was nothing you could have done," I tell him.

"I might have been able to stop him."

"You were nine."

"Or I could have calmed him down."

"You were *nine*." Even as I'm saying this, I can totally relate. I was only seven and I still regret that I didn't make

Mom sit down. Someone got up to give her their seat, but she told me to sit instead. We only had two more stops to go. If I had made her sit instead of me, I would have been the one standing. I would have been the one who got shoved. And our sister would be alive.

"That didn't register at the time," Marnix says. "When Dad took me to the hospital and I saw Mom lying there hooked up to machines, sobbing so hard the whole bed was shaking . . . all I could think about was that I should have been there. I was supposed to be there. The more I thought about it, the angrier I got. And after a while . . . I blamed myself for our sister never being born."

"It wasn't your fault."

"I know that now. Logically, anyway. But it still feels like my fault."

The sugary aroma of almond cookie rooibos tea wafts over us. My eyes sting with a surge of tears. I concentrate on smoothing my paper napkin against the rustic wooden table in slow strokes until my eyes dry up.

All these years, Marnix has been blaming himself for not being there.

All these years, I have been blaming myself for letting it happen.

We have both been blaming ourselves for something that was not our fault. For over ten years. And I had no freaking clue.

Now I understand why Marnix wanted to leave for

college so badly. He was trying to run away and not look back. Just like I was. He had his own nightmares haunting him.

Marnix stirs a packet of raw sugar into his coffee. "The anger and regret kept getting worse," he says. "At first it was just about her. Our sister we never knew."

Tears sting my eyes again. I smooth out my napkin some more.

"But then it snowballed into this crazy shit I couldn't control. By the time I was twelve or thirteen, I was regretting every single thing I should have said or should have done. I would replay the day in my room after school and imagine everything I wished had turned out differently. Stupid stuff I shouldn't have said to my friends. Giving the wrong answer in class. Missing an easy catch in gym. Just everything. My shrink thinks I could have benefited from meds. He says it sounds like I already had depression and anxiety issues, and that Mom's accident just made them worse. It was like a trigger that set everything off."

Like a trigger. That's exactly how I think about situations that make my bubbling anger boil over. I thought getting together with Marnix was going to be all about him, about what he needs and how I can help him recover. The last thing I expected was to discover more about myself.

"I couldn't stand to be alive," Marnix says.

This is horrible. Marnix was suffering for years and I

didn't even know it. I don't think our parents knew it, either. They assumed he was an angry teenager. As if teens are angry for no reason just because they're teens. Adults can be so dense sometimes. Now I realize that our mom was afraid to find out the truth and our dad got sick of the yelling matches. I suspect they were relieved when he left for college.

"The thing is," Marnix says, lifting his coffee mug and propping both elbows on the table, "no one can help you if you don't let them know you need help. Lashing out was my way of trying to get attention. I shut everyone out when I should have let you guys in. All those times I yelled at you and slammed my door in your face or pretended you didn't exist were to protect you from the truth. But I was stupid. I'm sorry I treated you that way. You deserved a brother who treated you better."

I've spent a lot of time thinking about the secret pain that exists within each one of us. The hurt that lurks behind every wall and window of this city has potential to connect us in profound ways. But we have to know where and what it is before we can help ease that pain. The secret pain Marnix has been carrying around with him is almost the same as mine. We have more in common than I ever knew.

Every single one of us has to fight against the darkness. I think we all have damaged parts of ourselves that we want to hide from the world. Some of us have to fight harder than others. But we all have to fight on. Positive energy is our best protection. My choice to create a positive lifestyle wasn't only a choice I made to counteract the negative. It was a choice that saved my life.

I will keep the promise I made last night with Rosanna and Darcy. I will become the truly optimistic person I want to be. I have the power to chase away the darkness lurking beneath my light. Of course I will encounter more hard times. There will always be challenges to overcome. That's just life. The important thing is how you choose to handle those challenges.

When I think about who my sister might have been, I want to have only warm feelings in my heart. No more anger. No more sadness.

"It's okay," I reassure my brother. "I should have made more of an effort to reach out to you."

"You did. I still have all your warm fuzzies."

"You do?"

"I keep them in my desk drawer. Every time I read them, I feel better."

I love that he kept the warm fuzzies I made for him in high school. I assumed he threw them out. Or ripped them up. It makes me happy knowing he still has them and that they are helping him a little.

Marnix tells me about college. I pepper him with questions about college life. He has lots of good advice. The more we talk, the more I realize he's not scary underneath his armor of anger. He is the Marnix I've always known on some level, the familiar brother I grew up with.

Marnix talks about therapy. His road to recovery will be a difficult journey, but he wants to love and accept himself. He wants to show the world who he truly is. And he wants to have a better relationship with me. With all of us. Family is who saved him . . . and who might save him again. He wants to be strong enough in case he ever has to save us.

After his coffee mug and my tea cup are empty, after the almond croissants we ordered later are gone, we sit at this window table in the neighborhood that will always belong to us and remember the good times from when we were little. Walking down Gay Street with Mom and running into a cluster of SantaCon participants all dressed in Christmas gear. Sneaking into Rocco's for butter cookies after school. Passing David Duchovny on the street enough times for him to feel like our neighbor instead of a famous actor. I could sit like this with Marnix for hours sharing our history.

Marnix gets serious again. "I want to be the brother I should have been all along," he says. "Can you ever forgive me?"

I meet his steady look so he knows I am equally serious. "I already have," I say.

I like the new Marnix and Sadie. On the other side. Where the possibilities are endless.

CHAPTER 29
DARCY

BIG BUBBLE GUY HAS TAKEN over Jude's spot.

This is the first time I've ever seen him, but I could not have given him a more perfect name. He's an older dude rocking cargo shorts, an ancient ribbed tank, and sneakers with white athletic socks halfway up his calves who's showing people how to make big bubbles. Right here in Washington Square Park where Jude used to perform. Buckets of soapy water are placed around him in a semicircle. Several sets of big bubble apparatus are lying on the ground. Each has two long sticks with some rope tied to the ends in a wide loop. Big Bubble Guy is showing everyone gathered around him how to dunk the rope end of the sticks in a bucket, then carefully lift the sticks up and slowly walk forward or backward to create enormous bubbles.

"It's weird seeing someone else in Jude's spot," I say.

Sadie and Rosanna nod. We only made our pact two nights ago, but I can tell they are already eager for some good news about me and Jude getting back together.

We watch Big Bubble Guy choose a little boy from the crowd as a volunteer. He helps the boy dunk the sticks in soapy water and hold them up. They take a few steps together, watching as a bubble forms. The bubble gets pretty big before it pops. This little kid should be proud. Instead he looks like he's going to cry over his popped bubble. So BBG tells him they are going to do something special. He positions the boy and tells him not to move. Then he identifies the boy's mother and tells her she might want to take a picture of this. BBG dips a set of sticks in a bucket, stands behind the boy facing away from him, then smoothly glides backward up to the boy and around him while holding the sticks out wide on either side of the boy. A massive bubble forms with the boy standing right in the middle. His mom takes pictures. The crowd cheers until the bubble bursts. Soap suds glide straight down like rain running down a window on either side of the boy, not touching him at all. Now the boy is laughing and clapping, his original popped bubble forgotten.

Jude makes little kids happy like that when he performs. It's like everything comes back to him.

"What time does the movie start?" I ask.

"Nine forty-five," Rosanna says. If you ever want to

know what time something starts, Rosanna is your girl. "We have over an hour."

Big Bubble Guy motions for us to join the fun. He doesn't have to ask me twice. I go over and pick up the only free set of sticks.

"Who wants to go first?" I hold them up for my girls, popping my hip like a game show hostess displaying a prize.

"You," Sadie says.

BBG is all excited as he coaches me on the best techniques to generate the largest bubbles. He reminds me of Jude again. They both love making other people happy by sharing what they are good at.

Sadie and Rosanna whoop at my first attempt, which is a big bubble that floats in the air for a few seconds. I do a few more before handing the sticks off to Sadie. A little girl's dad finishes with their sticks, putting them on the ground. Rosanna goes over to snag them. I suddenly get emotional watching Sadie and Rosanna making bubbles. I'm so thankful they are in my life. They have both come a long way this summer. We all have.

Big Bubble Guy isn't the only creative type in the park tonight. There's a boy around our age sitting right in the middle of the walkway sketching the Washington Square arch. The arch looks ethereal in its spotlights, stark white against the night sky. A group of eight people ranging from young to old is practicing meditation on the grass.

A band of two guys, one playing bagpipes and the other on drums, is jamming near the fountain. See, this is why I love it here. Where else can you find psychedelic Celtic rock on the street?

Mental note: Never leave New York. Except for vacays. If I can ever afford to take any. Which I will when I am a super successful publicist.

"Oh!" Sadie yells. I look over in time to see a gigantic bubble suspended between her sticks. Rosanna and I cheer until the bubble breaks free and floats up in the air.

After our fun with big bubbles, we sit on the edge of the fountain. I remember when I sat here at the beginning of the summer, all pissed over Logan dumping me right before I left California. Then I sat here with Logan after he supposedly came to win me back. Now I'm sitting here with my best friends. Water spraying upward dances in the lights that illuminate the fountain from below. That now familiar New York street smell of hot dogs and coffee is in the air. The park is packed with friends and lovers taking advantage of this warm summer night. I immerse myself in the Now, absorbing the enormity of this full-circle moment.

"I have something for both of you," Sadie says. She reaches into her small cotton bag printed with red and pink poppies.

"Pretty bag," I say approvingly.

"Thanks. It's new. I shoved all my ginormous bags in

the way back of my closet. Walking around with a small bag feels so much better."

"How do guys get away with not carrying a bag?" Rosanna wonders. "Do they just not take any stuff with them?"

"Girls have more stuff," I say.

"Why is that?"

"We put more effort into appearances."

"Only compared to boys who don't care how they look," Sadie points out. "There are plenty of boys who look way more fabulous than I ever will."

"Maybe. But girls are prepared for at least twenty-five types of minor emergencies at any given time."

"And some girls are prepared to distribute warm fuzzies." Sadie gives each of us warm fuzzies she made out of colored cardstock. I get a glittery gold star that says *Shine on, rock star.* Rosanna gets a red balloon that says *Go confidently in the direction of your dreams.*

"I love this!" Rosanna gushes. "Thank you!"

"How are you so awesome?" I ask Sadie.

"If by 'awesome' you mean 'dorky,' it just comes naturally."

"Warm fuzzies aren't dorky," Rosanna says. "They make the world a better place. *You* make the world a better place."

Sadie smiles her cutest aw-shucks grin. "We're all helping," she says.

I think again about how far we've come this summer.

We have grown closer to one another in two months than most of my friends and I ever did back in Santa Monica. Any day now we're supposed to hear from UNY if we can stay in our apartment for freshman year or if we will be transferred to other housing around campus. I really hope we get to stay together. Sadie and Rosanna have become my compass.

Across the fountain, the Celtic band finishes a song and tells us they are Scottish Octopus. People give them loud applause. No one can dispute that those guys rock. They roll into another song with lots of bagpipe trills and heavy drum action.

"So how's it going with our pact?" Sadie asks.

"I figured out my budget for freshman year," Rosanna reports. "No more bagels! Trader Joe's has all these pre-washed, pre-cut vegetables that aren't even expensive. I can afford to spend more on vegetables if I get them all there. They have kale, broccoli, green beans . . . all the good stuff."

"Just don't ask me to help you cook," I warn. "Unless you enjoy the smoke detector going off."

"Ooh, we need to get that replaced," Sadie says.

Rosanna continues. "You guys already know the Addison issue is over. Um . . . what was my third thing?"

"Reveling in your boy break," I remind her.

"Right. Still working on that." Rosanna turns to Sadie. "What about you?"

"Let's see. Talking with Marnix last night helped a lot. I was surprised that hearing how he's dealing with his baggage helped me unload mine. It's amazing. All this time we had so much in common and I had no idea."

Sadie watches the group meditating on the grass. We all watch them for a while. If anyone has mastered the art of being in the Now, it's them. They are completely focused despite all the city noise surrounding them. I want to block out distractions like they can. I have to learn how to be more focused on where my life is going. No one can help me anymore. I am the only one I can count on.

"Your turn," Sadie tells me.

Exactly.

"You mean have I convinced Jude we're meant to be together?" I quip. "Yeah, no, hasn't happened yet. But the cool thing is he's motivating me to be a better version of myself just by being himself. The first time I went to his office, I couldn't believe what I was seeing. Here was a street magician who transformed himself into a super successful entrepreneur. It was like the most magnificent magic trick ever. But Jude earned everything he has all by himself. He didn't take money from his parents. He didn't mooch off anyone. His success is all his own."

I look up at the arch illuminated against the night sky, strong and stable. I want to be like that. I want to be impressive, someone people can look up to. Maybe even a role model. I don't want to fall back into bad habits. Every time I think about Jude's success, I realize all over again how drastically I am not living up to my own potential. He makes me want to be everything I can be.

Being with someone who inspires you to be a better person is an excellent sign that they are right for you.

I cannot believe what an idiot I was. How could I have let Jude slip away? Was Summer Fun Darcy so determined to have boy adventures that she couldn't see what was right in front of her? Jude wanted a committed relationship. I wanted to keep things light and fun. I refused to let another boy hurt me again, and at the time I thought Jude was just another boy. But he wasn't. He's not. Jude would never hurt me the way Logan did. It's just not who he is.

All boys are not created equal.

This epiphany was not easy to come by. I didn't think I was capable of wanting another committed relationship after Logan. Until I was. And then I started to think about something I'd never considered before.

What if it's not them? What if it's me?

Logan was a first-class dumbass. No question. But what if there's something about me that makes me more inclined to be attracted to boys like Logan? The sexy sloucher bad boys that no girl's daddy wants her bringing home. The ones who will inevitably break her heart.

I woke up when I met Jude. It just took me a while to see that.

I want to know what it's like to be in the kind of love

that inspires you to look into yourself and follow your heart without fear. You have to go all in to bet on that kind of real love. No bluffing. No folding. No losing faith in your cards.

Emotional walls don't protect you. They prevent you from living your best life.

Jude has to know my true feelings. That I want to be with him for real, the way he wants me to be. I will make better choices now to create the future I want.

A future with Jude in it. If it's not too late.

CHAPTER 30
ROSANNA

"WHY DON'T WE START WITH why you're here?"
Dr. Ribisi suggests.

So far I like therapy. Dr. Ribisi has a very calming presence. Her voice is smooth and low. I could probably live
in her office. It's just as chill as she is with its neutral color
scheme, fuzzy cream pillows on the big almond-colored
couch, and bookshelves displaying a pleasing balance of
books and arty objects. Her office is in a new building for
different medical specialties on the UNY campus. Fortunately my student health insurance covers sessions with
psychologists.

"Okay," I begin. "I had my first boyfriend this summer.
Donovan. D. We're not together anymore. We broke up."

"Who broke up with whom?"

"Technically I did? But it was because he was in love

with someone else. He just didn't know it. He was really good to me, though. We . . ." I twist my hands in my lap, trying to figure out what to say next. How to say it. "I was afraid to move forward with him. Physically. I was molested when I was eleven and . . . I thought that was why."

Dr. Ribisi's expression doesn't change. She looks open and interested to hear what I have to say. Dr. Ribisi has perfect posture in her big armchair, even with her legs crossed. She writes something down in the notebook balanced on her thigh.

"Could that have been why?" I ask.

Dr. Ribisi looks at me. "Maybe. Or maybe you were cautious because he wasn't the right person for you."

Whoa. How have I never thought of that? It totally makes sense. Just because D was a good guy who took care of me doesn't mean he was right for me. How could I have ever felt comfortable with him physically if his heart belonged to someone else?

"What else has been on your mind?" Dr. Ribisi asks.

I let everything pour out. "I'm trying to work on not being afraid. I couldn't wait to move to New York, but it's been scary. I worry about money every day. My parents can't afford to help me pay for college. New York is way more expensive than I thought it would be and I've been worried about paying for everything. Next week I'll barely be scraping by. Tomorrow is my last day as a camp counselor and I don't start my work-study job until fall semester begins." One of the fuzzy throw pillows is sitting next to me on the couch. It looks really soft. Am I allowed to touch it? Can I put it on my lap?

"How did you like being a camp counselor?"

"I loved it. I had a group of eight-year-old girls who were adorable. We had a lot of fun. Except for . . . a girl in my group was being abused by her mom's boyfriend." I tell Dr. Ribisi about Momo, about reporting my suspicions to Frank, who did nothing, and about finding Momo trapped in that horrible crawl space. "I don't know why Frank never did anything. He's probably just a typical administrator . . . too lazy to do the right thing. I mean, most people don't do anything when they see a problem, unless it's directly related to them. Frank knows that I found Momo in her apartment, but he hasn't talked to me about it. Not even to apologize." Why Frank wouldn't investigate will probably remain a mystery forever.

"You said you're working on not being afraid," Dr. Ribisi says. "Are you afraid of anything else?"

"Mice. We had mice before and now I'm paranoid a mouse is going to claw its way up into my bed while I'm sleeping. Before I go into my room at night, I turn on the light and wait a few seconds in the doorway to check if a mouse is running across the floor."

"The joys of city living."

"More seriously, though . . . when I first got here, I was

afraid of being alone. Like if something bad happened and I didn't have my family or friends to help me. But now I have Sadie and Darcy. And Mica again. That's a long story."

Dr. Ribisi smiles. "Then it's a good thing we have time."

CHAPTER 31

SADIE

IMPERIAL WOODPECKER SNO-BALLS IS THE only place I want to be on a sweltering night like this. Their air-conditioning is almost as cold as their shaved ice.

Austin and I grabbed the only free table when we got here. When some people left, he swiftly relocated two more chairs to our table. We needed them for Vienna and Jesse.

The only time I had ever seen Vienna before tonight was at our annual Remembrance Walk. She always said she wanted to get together in real life. But the concept of interacting with her outside of our insulated bubble scared me. I thought that if I didn't have to see Vienna outside of the walk, I could restrict my mourning to that one day a year. But that's not how things turned out. My nightmares are a warning sign that I have to face the loss of my sister. The loss refuses to be restricted to one day a year. It is with me all the time. The only way to heal this hole in my heart is to expose what happened. Hiding pain gives it even more power. I can't risk the darkness taking over my life like it did to Marnix.

Vienna was really surprised when I called her. She didn't think I ever would. Neither did I. Asking Vienna to be part of my real life was a huge step. I felt like I had to reach out to her as part of the pact I made with Rosanna and Darcy. I'm not as worried about explaining how I know Vienna now that Austin, Darcy, and Rosanna all know about my sister.

After I ran into Jesse in the laundry room again, I wasn't ready to call Vienna about that party even though I said I would. Telling Darcy about the party was just an excuse. I was afraid to see Vienna. So I thought I could make it up to Jesse and bring Vienna into my life at the same time. Last time I saw her at the walk, Vienna said she liked a good friend of hers but was too afraid to tell him how she really felt. She eventually told him, but he didn't feel the same way. So here we are.

"What about melon and root beer?" Jesse asks Vienna.

Vienna ponders this combination. They are figuring out which sno-ball flavors on the menu could be mixed to make the best new flavors.

"That just might be radical enough to work," Vienna decides. "Birthday cake marshmallow?"

"Too sweet."

"Hello, that's the point."

"Maybe coconut marshmallow?"

"But then it would be all white," Vienna objects. "What fun is all white shaved ice? Where's the party in my container?"

"You could have a party with rainbow sprinkles on top," Jesse offers. He takes a huge bite of his spearmint sno-ball.

"There you go." Vienna smiles at me. "You didn't tell me the boy was a genius."

"Only when it comes to sno-balls," Jesse says. "And laundry." He winks at Vienna. Her smile turns into a goofy grin.

"Want to try?" Austin holds up a spoonful of his blackberry for me. It would totally go with my cherry, but I'm trying not to be that couple. The couple who acts all adorable feeding each other and makes you want to gag. Normally I wouldn't care what other people think, but I don't want to make Vienna and Jesse uncomfortable with our googly eyes. Even though they're acting just as googly.

I take the spoon from Austin. The intense blackberry flavor bursts in my mouth. Austin beams at me. He can tell I am savoring this flavor. He loves making me happy with the little things.

Austin and I were floating in a love bubble when we first got together. I fell for him so fast I couldn't even think straight. But I had been waiting forever for a soul mate to come into my life. And then there he was, bright as day, undeniable. I knew we were meant to be.

Our love bubble popped when I found out he was married. When Shirley showed up at my building and then made that scene at the Slipper Room, I got scared that this would be my life if I stayed with Austin. A life of constantly looking over my shoulder for his stalker ex. Shirley rattled me to the core at the Slipper Room. I was determined to appear strong, but inside I was terrified. When Austin and I talked after, I told him that I might want to take a break until she calmed down and they were officially divorced. But Rosanna told me how humiliated Shirley was when they went outside. Rosanna doesn't think Shirley will come after us again.

This ex situation has been complicated. I didn't sign up for this. My soul mate didn't come in the package I was expecting. But I fell in love with Austin unconditionally. If I want us to stay together, I have to accept all of him, just like he has to accept all of me.

Everything happens for a reason. There is a reason I ran into Jesse in the laundry room again. Bringing Jesse and Vienna together could lead to a magnificent chain of events that all began because I was twenty-five cents short on my laundry card. You never know when a non-coincidence can change your life.

Austin pulls my chair over so it's touching his. He puts his arm around me and I rest my head against his shoulder, watching Vienna and Jesse mix their spearmint and lemon flavors together. They are exuding that blissful euphoria you feel when you're falling in like with someone. I can hear it in the way Vienna laughs at Jesse's jokes like he's the funniest boy in the world. I can see it in Jesse's eyes when he looks at Vienna, attracted and intrigued. Times like this make me appreciate the beauty of how everything is connected. All the choices we make—every action, every word, every thought—have an impact on the world around us in ways more profound than we could ever imagine.

We all make mistakes. We all have regrets we wish we could go back and do over. But wallowing in those regrets is not living. Life is about believing that we can do better next time. And never losing hope that maybe, if we refuse to give up, we will become the person we actually want to be.

CHAPTER 32
DARCY

I'M FLYING ON A NATURAL high as I sail across campus from the UNY Academic Resource Center. One of the freshman academic advisers gave me information on declaring a major within the Department of Media, Culture, and Communication. My bag is filled with brochures, pamphlets, and notes that will become components of my road map to success. Never thought I'd see the day, but I love being a girl with a road map.

It blows my mind how quickly life can turn around after a bomb shatters your entire world. One day you think there is no possible way things will ever get better. It seems like you will always feel this broken, this devastated, this desperate. But then you force yourself to keep going. You make plans to pull yourself out of the rubble. You pick yourself up, dust yourself off, and start over. That's when life meets you halfway and mighty forces help to make things happen.

A peace I've never felt before engulfs me like one of those big bubbles in the park. Like no matter what else life throws at me, it will all be okay. I will make it okay.

The campus is empty, but I can almost feel the nervous excitement from students who will be flooding in next week for fall semester. Almost like I'm picking up on the energy of everyone who can't wait to come back to college or arrive for the first time. Could this be part of the whole creative visualization thing Sadie's been talking about? She's reading this book all about visualizing your dream life, then making that vision reality. Listening to her worship the power of positive energy sounded more like cult brainwashing and less like practical advice at first. But now I think she's on to something.

When I was describing my mental picture of my future to the adviser, it made me feel powerful. Not only because I am determined to build a new life for myself on my own. Because I could feel the strength my thoughts have in building that life. Sadie says that our thoughts influence our words, our words influence our actions, and our actions shape our lives. Now I understand what she means. I used to think girl power was mostly about sisterhood. Also about taking a stand and being your best self. Being confident enough to own your choices, to chase after what makes you happy even if others don't agree. I have always followed my heart in that way. But now I'm beginning to understand how much power my thoughts have. Sadie is right. Positive thoughts do result in positive actions. Just in case she's also right about that feng shui stuff, I moved two of the glass bottles that were on my dresser to my windowsill facing south. Objects in pairs along a southern wall allegedly promote relationship prosperity.

Daydreams about Jude sneak into my thoughts as I walk to Bleecker Street. Instead of visualizing me telling him I want to be his girlfriend and him shutting me down, I visualize the most positive scene I can imagine. I tell Jude I want to be his girlfriend. He sweeps me up in his arms and tells me I'm the only girl for him. He says some cliché movie line like "What took you so long?" And then we have this epic kiss in front of a huge window high above our city, glittery lights sparkling below us.

I would never admit how happy this cheesy fantasy is making me.

I walk past my dream apartment before realizing I didn't even notice it. Which is crazy because I always stop to look inside. That's how powerful my Jude movie kiss fantasy was. Or maybe it's because I actually made it to the other side of the glass. I love this apartment more than ever, but its lure isn't as strong as it was before. I have seen what's on the other side. That sense of wonder, standing here all those times filling in the blanks, is what pulled me in. Finding my way to the other side of the glass is now another sweet memory I can add to my first summer in New York.

A new glittery rose-gold Kate Spade bag winks at me from the window of this boutique I adore on Bleecker Street. I wink back. Then I go inside. Raoul is on the floor, fussing over an immaculate display of Dolce & Gabbana clutches. Each one shimmers in its own fabulous way.

I dart over to Raoul, my fave sales associate. "Did these just come in?" I drool.

"New this morning." He holds up a shiny silver clutch with a mirrored clasp for my admiration. "Aren't they to die?"

"Want." Old Darcy would have snatched up this clutch in a flash along with the metallic gold one perched next to it. But New Darcy doesn't even touch them. Instead I slip behind the counter and take over the register. This is so much better than working at Java Stop.

I didn't just want a new job at one of my favorite boutiques in the Village. I needed this job. One more day at Java Stop and I would have had a meltdown all over the chocolate croissants. Making those ridiculously pretentious coffee drinks was not the best use of my social butterfly skills or wealth of fashion knowledge. So I totally stalked this place and a bunch of other boutiques I love. I kept calling the managers. I stopped by before and after my Java Stop shifts, chatting up the salespeople for inside information. Turns out there was a position opening up here because the girl who had this job before me left for grad school in Ohio. I nabbed the opening before it was even listed.

According to Raoul, summer Friday afternoons can be busy with tourists. But today is kind of slow. I make sure all the clothing pieces are facing the same way on the hangers. I rearrange the shoe display so the highest heels are on the top risers. I daydream about Jude some more behind the counter, watching people outside trudge along in the sticky heat. Then I call my mom on my break at the pizza place across the street.

"Are you loving the new job?" she asks.

"You know I am. But I didn't call to talk about me. How are you doing?"

"Taking it one day at a time. It's good to spend more time with Grandma. She likes having me around."

Mom tells me about the communal gardening they're doing and the dinners they're cooking and the movies they're watching. Her voice sounds strong, but I know she is forcing herself to put on a brave face for me. Mom is moving past those awful conversations where I could hear her crying. She's probably embarrassed that she was so exposed in front of me. Her life is completely different now, even more different than mine.

Last time we talked, I was asking Mom about her support system. I wanted to know what her friends have been doing to help her through this impossible time. After heavy prodding, she admitted that she hasn't been invited to the social engagements she used to go to a few times a week. No more dinner parties. No more fund-raising events. The group of women she usually plays bridge with "forgot" to tell her who was hosting their next game. Women she thought were her friends won't return her calls. They are treating Mom like her bad luck is contagious. Or as if they don't believe she had nothing to do with the tax fraud. It's like she's being ostracized for what my father did. It's so unfair. He cheats and breaks the law, but she's the one who is paying the price. Meanwhile he's living large in his extravagant new house with his new family.

One good thing about having your life turned upside down is you get to find out who your real friends are. Mom is devastated that women she has known for years are acting like she doesn't exist. At least she can count on me and Grandma for support. Just like I know I can count on them. I'm lucky to also have Sadie and Rosanna in my life. If they showed me anything when they found out about my father, it's that they will stick by me no matter what.

My break is almost over. I try to think of some comforting words that will convince Mom she has nothing to worry about. But how can she not worry? How will she be able to afford a new home? What will she do with her life? Does she want to get married again, or is she swearing off serious relationships like I did when summer started?

What if she ends up alone?

"Well, I guess I'll let you get back to work," Mom says. "I'm meeting some new friends for coffee."

"You have new friends?"

"Exciting, right? I met three women who get together at this cute café in the neighborhood most weekday afternoons. They're all full-time moms. Their kids are younger than you, but we have so much in common. They've been asking me for all sorts of advice. I love talking to them. It's nice to feel useful outside of work."

"Do they know about . . . ?"

"They know all about your father and they have been extremely kind. They don't see me as damaged goods. They see me as someone with experience who can offer guidance. I'm so grateful I found them."

"That's awesome, Mom."

"One of them even hired me to cater her husband's birthday party. Grandma wants to help us with the cooking. It's a big job."

My mom is working it like a boss. Not only is she refusing to be a victim, she is rebuilding her life. She gets to start from scratch and design a new life that looks more like who she actually wants to be. Who she actually is. She can connect with new people who understand where she's coming from. Even if they can't relate directly to what she's going through, good people will sympathize and help her find her way. Not like those plastic socialite wives who only wanted to know her when she had money.

Maybe this new life she's building on her own will make her happier than her old life. Which would make total sense. How happy can you be if your life is a lie?

My mom doesn't have to live a lie anymore. She set herself free.

CHAPTER 33
ROSANNA

TODAY WAS THE LAST DAY of camp. Saying goodbye to all my campers was hard. But I was choking back tears when I said goodbye to Momo. She made me promise to be pen pals with her so we will still know everything about each other next summer. I am already looking forward to next summer when I'll be a counselor again and Momo will be back at camp. Frank said I could be a counselor to a group of nine-year-old girls, most of whom I had this summer. He didn't say anything about Momo directly. But the way he said thank you before we left seemed like he was thanking me for more than just working here.

So I'm kind of in limbo. I have a free week before classes start. One week to get my books and supplies, figure out a running schedule I can realistically stick to, and plan my budget and meals. My goal is to do grocery shopping at

Trader Joe's every weekend. That way I can pack healthy lunches for the week every Sunday so I'm ready to go.

Now I have a whole weekend ahead of me to enjoy the magic of New York City. I'm buzzing with anticipation. The three of us are having a party on our roof this weekend. We invited everyone we know. Sadie and I are in charge of snacks. Darcy is on decorations. But tonight is all mine. Since it's broiling out, I have decided this will be a night to stay in, keep cool, and clean my room. I put on a playlist starting with "Ziggy Stardust." The shell that D found on the beach for me during our sunset walk in South Beach catches my eye. I stuck it on my windowsill when I got home. I pick up the shell, brushing my fingers over its smooth surface, tracing the light-pink lines against the white background. Then I put the shell away in the jewelry box Momo gave me. It is proudly displayed on my dresser, already filling up with fun jewelry Darcy has been helping me find on sale.

Next I take all my bags out of the closet and put them on my bed. I turn each of them over, emptying their contents of stray change, hair bands, pens, lip balm, Band-Aids, tissues, and various scraps. I unfold the paper scraps to make sure they are not important. One paper is folded into a tiny square. It was stashed so deep inside my bag it didn't even fall out at first.

I unfold the tiny square of paper. It's the ATM receipt from when I took money out on the way to my first date with D. The one that said I only had seventy-three cents left. In the whole world. My heart hammers with the same fear I felt looking at this receipt for the first time. I stare at the receipt as if it is telling my fortune. But the seventy-three cents incident is part of my past. Not my future. I have student loans coming in for tuition and a work-study job that will cover my housing and food. The concept of affording to live here for at least four years is still scary, but I am a lot less afraid than I was two months ago.

My first instinct is to crumple up the receipt and chuck it in the garbage. But I actually want to save it. This receipt will be a reminder of the strength I sometimes forget I have. I survived having only seventy-three cents in New York City. I did not give up, turn around, and go home. I kept moving forward, determined to succeed. And I did.

I hang the receipt on my bulletin board with a pushpin. My walls don't have that much on them. I'm waiting to hear if we are staying before I put more up. My favorite thing on the wall was a print my grandma sent me for graduation. Now it's the red balloon warm fuzzy Sadie made for me. I put it above my bed to match the RIGHT AROUND THE CORNER sign Sadie has above her bed. Darcy put her gold star warm fuzzy on her door like a dressing room.

My red balloon says GO CONFIDENTLY IN THE DIRECTION OF YOUR DREAMS. Sadie didn't just select that quote for its dream big motivation. She knows

I want to be more confident. I wonder if I seem any more confident than I did when we met at the beginning of the summer. I get that I still look like someone who fell off the hay truck from the Midwest. But I'm trying to project enough confidence to blend in with the real New Yorkers. Sometimes I feel like I am, like when I'm walking down the street with a surge of people, one of many in the crowd. Or when I'm standing in a long line at the post office, enduring with the natives. I can't wait for the day when I completely feel at home here. Like I am finally a real New Yorker. I know that day is inevitable, because this is where I belong.

I want to build confidence in so many areas of my life. When I become confident, I will have confidence in my relationships, too. I used to think I was unworthy of D because I came from nothing. Because I am broken. But Dr. Ribisi pointed out that I didn't come from nothing. I came from a good home with extremely hardworking parents who supported me as much as they could. That's more than a lot of kids can say. When Dr. Ribisi said that, she helped me understand that I am worthy. I am capable of putting the broken pieces of my life back together.

I've also been thinking about why I was afraid to move forward physically with D. I think Dr. Ribisi was right about him not being the right person for me. I used to think that when you are with the right person, they don't make you feel jealous or suspicious or unworthy. But that's not really it. When you are ready to be with the right person, you don't make yourself feel that way.

Turns out I wasn't ready for a serious relationship. Not when there was so much I was anxious about, so much that needed to be resolved. I won't consider another serious relationship again until I have had enough therapy to work through the consequences of my sexual abuse, and work on accepting myself for who I am. I have to feel worthy of the kind of relationship I want before I can have it. So here I am. At the end of my past life and the beginning of my shiny new one.

On the verge of everything.

CHAPTER 34

SADIE

RIGHT AROUND THE CORNER . . .

. . . can be possibilities beyond your wildest dreams.

. . . can be discoveries you didn't even know you were looking for.

. . . can be roommates who turn out to be your best friends.

The three of us had been waiting to hear from UNY Housing if we would get to stay in this apartment freshman year. The email came this morning:

Dear Sadie,

The University of New York is pleased to inform you that your request to retain your current summer housing assignment has been approved. The enclosed documents contain details of your extended housing agreement for the upcoming fall and spring semesters.

On behalf of the Department of Student Housing, welcome to your freshman year!

Darcy and Rosanna must have received the same email. Earlier this summer, we all requested to stay together.

The first thing I did when I read my email was bust out in a dorky happy dance in my room.

That was not nearly enough celebration.

I ran to Rosanna's room. She was awake, but she hadn't read her email yet. We both squealed and jumped around when she read it. Darcy wasn't awake yet. We went to Waverly Diner for brunch to celebrate and figure out what snacks we're making for our rooftop party tomorrow night.

There's even more good news. Austin found an apartment. A renovated one without a bathtub in the kitchen. He's moving on August 31. I'm going to Trey's place to help him pack. I just came home after brunch so I could grab some clothes and things for tomorrow. I'll probably spend the night there . . . but not like when Austin slept over here. Austin said he understood if I wanted to sleep on the couch. As crazy as that would have sounded a month ago and as hard as it's going to be to stick to later tonight, it might be the smartest choice.

We have been talking a lot since Shirley's crash stalking

at the Slipper Room. I had an idea that we could start over. Take things slow. Get to know each other gradually instead of falling head over heels in love so fast I couldn't see what was coming. We both want to be together for a long time. Maybe even forever. Which means our relationship has to have a solid foundation for us to build the future we want. So we're taking the intensity down a notch. Just long enough to share the truth about who we were, who we are, and who we want to be.

I open my closet door. Taking an inventory of my smaller bags, I select the smallest bag that will fit everything I want to take with me tonight. Then some inspiration strikes. I snatch a black Sharpie from the glass of pens on my desk and inspect the walls of my closet. On the right wall close to the door I write: *Sadie was here.* Even though we're staying here this year, I want to make sure a part of me stays here forever. Living here has been so much more than the escape I thought it would be. No matter how many apartments I end up renting, or maybe even buying, I will never forget my first. No matter how many divergent paths the three of us follow, or how much distance may come between us, I will always carry Darcy and Rosanna in my heart.

This summer was about loving ourselves. About becoming the girls we wanted to be for so long. When the summer began, we had no idea we would be helping each other work through the pain of everything we were running from. We did not expect to form a bond of sister-hood that just might last forever.

The essence of city love this summer wasn't about boys. It was about the three of us.

CHAPTER 35
DARCY

SO THAT NIGHT JUDE CAME over when Logan showed up? The night he had something special planned?

He was going to take me to One World Observatory.

That's why we're here now. Jude still wanted to take me even after I blew it the first time.

We have already scoped out the full 360-degree views of the observation floor. Settling in at a window facing north so we can see almost all of Manhattan was the obvious choice.

"Remember when you said this would be a night I'd never forget?" I ask Jude as we're looking out across our city, sparkling in the twilight. We're pressed up against the glass with our arms touching, gold glitter city lights stretching out below us. Standing so close to him, watching the sky grow dark . . . it feels like we're floating above the world.

Jude doesn't look away from the view. "Yeah?"

"You were right."

"Oh yes. I was."

We watch the city come alive as night rolls in. My arm burns against his. What would he do if I tried to hold his hand? Would he let me? Or would he reiterate that we're just friends?

Sadie always says how anything is possible in New York. Could it be possible that Jude still wants to be with me? Is it possible that he's been missing me this whole time? And that tonight is his way of starting again? Imagining Jude wanting to be with me when we were apart reminds me of these song lyrics. They play in my head:

I'm here without you baby,
but you're still with me in my dreams.
And tonight it's only you and me.

Jude turns to look at me, his body still pressed against the glass. His arm still pressed against mine. Why wouldn't he move his arm unless he wanted it there?

"What?" he says.

"What?"

"Why were you looking at me?"

"Was I?"

Jude seems like he's going to say something else. Then he goes back to looking out across the city.

There is a chance we can have something real. I know it. But not until I tell him everything.

I clear my throat. "I guess . . . I wanted to tell you something. Something big." My heart is pounding so hard I actually have to catch my breath.

"Okay . . ." Jude turns so his shoulder is leaning against the glass. I back up against a pillar we're standing next to. Our extreme height above the world suddenly hits me. Maybe that's why I feel dizzy.

The best way to say it is to just say it.

I take a deep breath. "My dad had an affair. And committed tax fraud. We have no money left. Now he's living with the other woman and my mom had to move in with my grandma."

Jude's mouth falls open.

People cluster around us in waves as I tell Jude about the past few weeks. Tourists speaking different languages weave in and out of our conversation. Families pose their kids in front of the window for pictures. Couples show off their relationships with deep kisses.

I hate them as much as I want to be them.

"Why didn't you tell me all this before?" Jude asks.

"You had just let me back into your life. I didn't want to push you away again with my insane family drama. Seeing your office and how successful you were . . . I felt even worse about how my life was turning out. I know it sounds horrible. I just wanted us to be like we were."

Jude pushes off the glass. "You mean . . . when we were together?"

I nod. I can't speak. If I speak and say too much and he doesn't feel the same way, I will crumble into a million pieces of mortification.

Jude takes a step closer to me. We're almost touching again. But this time he slips his hands around my waist, locking his eyes with mine.

"As you wish," he says.

As you wish. *Princess Bride* speak for *I love you.*

I remember this. The magnetic pull he always had on me right before he kissed me. The sweet anticipation of the kiss was almost as good as the kiss itself.

This time is no different. Except when he kisses me this time, I remember my epic movie kiss fantasy. Me telling Jude how I feel. Him saying he feels the same way. Then kissing me in front of a huge window overlooking our city.

And now we are here.

We are here.

CHAPTER 36
ROSANNA

"OH!" SADIE POINTS FAR IN the distance beyond our rooftop. The sky is illuminated in fluttery pulses. We watch until the pulses fade away. "I love heat lightning."

"Same here." I look up at the night sky, a shade I have come to recognize as New York City purple. Only three stars are visible that might not even be stars. I think they are planets. But an old sense of comfort settles in as a new song comes on and the people at our rooftop party talk, laugh, dance, and eat the snacks Sadie and I made this afternoon. The stars are still there even when I can't see them. I don't need them to guide me anymore. A bright new inner light is guiding my way.

"What did I miss?" Darcy perches on the edge of my lawn chair. Sadie is sitting in a matching chair next to mine. There is nothing fancy about our rooftop. It's as old-school as a rooftop can get with its uneven tar patches, lack of vegetation, and random outdoor furniture apparently left behind when people moved out. A cheap pine deck chair broke when Marnix sat on it. He played it off like it was all on purpose. I love his sense of humor. Maybe Darcy and I will get to know him better, since Marnix decided to take the fall semester off to concentrate on his recovery.

"Heat lightning," I tell Darcy.

"Damn. I miss all the good stuff. Do we—"

"Look!" Sadie yells, pointing in the distance again.

The heat lightning is back. We watch it throb and flicker, mesmerized.

"See that stripy lights building in Jersey City?" Sadie asks us. She points across the river to New Jersey. "The one with the slanted top and the purple and blue light stripes blinking?"

"Yes!" I say. "That's so cool."

"I have wondered what those stripes mean for years. Every night they're different colors. Some nights they're just solid white. Some nights there aren't any lights at all." Sadie's face lights up brighter than the stripes. "Austin found out what they mean for me."

"Zombie apocalypse warnings?" Darcy ventures.

"Close. They follow weather patterns."

"I like the zombie thing better."

"Do we what?" I ask Darcy.

"Hmmm?"

"You were asking—"

"Right. Do we have any more sugar cookies? Tomer wants to try one."

I love that Darcy invited her fantasy apartment boy.

"All gone as of an hour ago," Sadie reports.

Tomer is talking to Carrie, Jude, and Austin. It was cool of Darcy to invite Carrie. I loved Darcy's "big city, small world" story of running into Carrie on the Upper West Side a year after they met on a train from Milan to Monaco. Carrie isn't the only "big city, small world" example up on the roof tonight. It turns out Jesse is D's friend from high school. I recognized him tonight from one time when I watched them playing basketball. I guess D didn't realize Jesse lived in my building. In the apartment right below ours. Carrie says these kinds of connections happen all the time here, but that is incredible. New York really is a magical place for bringing people together, whether they are new soul mates or old friends reuniting on a random street corner years later.

Jude comes over to us. He lifts Darcy up and twirls her around in a circle. She giggles in delight. Then he gently puts her back down and kisses her. They walk hand in hand to where Mica and Brooke are dancing. This is Brooke's last summer rooftop experience before she leaves for college tomorrow.

It's funny how Darcy used to annoy me. Now I admire

her. Darcy has been pushed, tested, and manipulated, but she has overcome every one of her challenges. Now she is stronger than ever.

Sadie sighs. "Could we be swooning any harder that Jarcy is back?"

"Jarcy?" I make a face at the weak smoosh name. "Is that the best we can do?"

Sadie thinks. "Dude!"

I wait to hear what she came up with. She doesn't say anything.

"What?" I ask.

"Dude is their better name!"

She looks so excited she makes me laugh. Both names are pretty bad.

I inhale the summery scents of flowers from the landscaped rooftop next door. My stomach is trembling with nervous excitement for college. I am already overwhelmed by the new home I have made and the new people in my life. I am dazzled by how much I love my new home.

I used to think I would always be at the mercy of external variables. But although there are lots of things I can't control, I can control my reaction to them. I can choose to not be afraid.

Vienna whoops when Beyoncé comes on. She grabs Jesse and they start dancing. They move in sync like they've been together for years. Everyone else joins in.

Sadie looks at me. "Want to dance?"

"I want to just watch for a minute," I say. "But you should go."

"No. I like watching our people with you."

We have people here. I have people here.

Sadie and I watch our people dancing. Jude holding Darcy close even though it's a fast song. Austin doing disco moves to make Sadie laugh. Vienna and Jesse stealing the show. Mica, Brooke, Marnix, Tomer, and Carrie having a dance off. My heart swells with happiness and gratitude that I am not alone in my dream city. Anything is possible in New York City. Even things they told you were impossible.

Sometimes when I talk to family or friends back home, I can tell they don't understand about the magical energy of New York City. Some people don't understand how I knew this was my true home years before I got here. Or the way this city makes me feel alive every single day. That's okay. I don't expect them to. But I try to explain it like this: It's like that feeling you get when you meet the love of your life. You can feel that way about a place, too. It's a feeling that means you are home. I don't know when I will fall in love again. But I know that I will be forever in love with New York City and the infinite possibilities it brings.

Darcy dashes over to us holding three cups of watermelon juice. She perches on the edge of my chair again and gives cups to Sadie and me.

"Toast time!" she trumpets.

We all raise our cups.

"To girl power," Sadie says.

"To sisterhood," Darcy says.

"To city love," I say.

This toast feels like another pact to me. This time, our promise is to move forward together.

We are all those things. And there is so much more to come.

To us.

ACKNOWLEDGMENTS

AS I WRITE THESE ACKNOWLEDGMENTS in August 2016, I am celebrating my 20th New Yorkiversary. I moved here in the middle of a blizzard on January 6, 1996, to start grad school at New York University, determined to turn my big dreams into reality. Twenty years later, I am living the life I envisioned all those years ago. That's the magic of New York City. Anything is possible.

Taking on a trilogy is an enormous endeavor for a publisher, and I am forever in love with the HarperCollins team who made the City Love trilogy happen. My legendary editor and publisher, Katherine Tegen, is a role model for creating a dream life. My rock star publicist, Rosanne Romanello, works it and owns it like a boss. Thanks to Alana Whitman, marketing genius, and Lauren Flower, professional book pusher. Erin Fitzsimmons designed the most gorgeous covers for this trilogy. And the Epic Reads group is actually beyond epic. These fierce and fabulous women of the publishing world brought *City Love*, *Lost in Love*, and *Forever in Love* to life. It has been an honor to work with them for the past three years.

Infinite thanks to my readers for making this life possible. You are why I write.

Heart-kiss emojis to the librarians, teachers, bloggers, and everyone else who spread the city love with warm fuzzies about this trilogy. You connect readers to books, and for that I am forever grateful.

My fiancé, Matt, and his family have opened a new chapter in my life, a chapter I had never read before but always hoped would be part of my story one day. Go, karma.

The sparkly city lights who influenced this trilogy over the years deserve to be showered with glittery confetti. Jim Downs, plaque pact partner. Mike Ippoliti, Anton Yarovoy, and Laila Dadvand, High Line enthusiasts. Joe Torello, who works the Feast of San Gennaro like nobody's business. Kara Doyle, whose positive energy, killer choreo, and dedication to fitness for life inspire me every day. Stephen Venters, who had plans with me to go to the Twin Towers on September 11, 2001. Tim Stockert, for driving the U-Haul that moved me from Philadelphia to New York in that blizzard. And of course, New York City, my first and forever city love.

READ THEM ALL NOW!

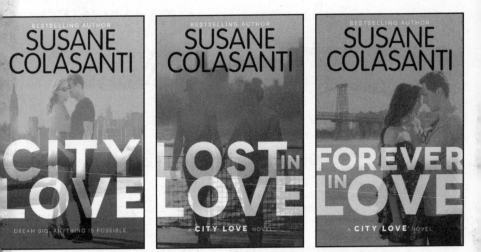

DREAM BIG.
ANYTHING IS POSSIBLE.